STOV

FRIENDS
OF ACPL

Katzimo,
Mysterious Mesa

KATZIMO, MYSTERIOUS MESA

Bobette Gugliotta

Illustrated by Lorence F. Bjorklund

DODD, MEAD & COMPANY   New York

Dedicated to Arthur Bibo

Author's Note U. S.1803654

This book is based upon the lives of Juana and Solomon Bibo. It is not a history of the family but a story woven from selected strands. The bulk of the material is derived from tape recordings made with Arthur Bibo, Carl Bibo, Harold Bibo in New Mexico, Helen Vallo (at the pueblo of Ácoma in New Mexico), Keith Lummis and Leo Bibo in California.

The ancient lands of Ácoma belong to the Quéres group of pueblos which also include Santa Ana, San Felipe, Santo Domingo, Zia, Cochití, and Laguna. Although there might be slight differences in phraseology, these seven nations speak the same root language, Quéresan, which differs radically from the languages of other tribes of New Mexico such as the Zuñi, Navaho, Hopi, and others. The Quéres Indians claim the range of the Tanos Mountains, the valleys of the upper Rio Grande and the Jémez rivers as their ancient heritage.

Contents

7

1

The Man Who
Climbed Katzimo

Carl Bibo had just eased one leg over the bannister and was about to enjoy the forbidden slide down when he heard a terrific pounding on the front door and a deep voice booming out.

"Open up! Open up, and be quick about it."

Jumping off, Carl crouched down and peered through the balustrade wondering if he should answer or leave it to someone better able to cope with such a command than a thirteen-year-old boy. Then he caught sight of his mother, Juana, walking with measured tread, her expression unperturbed as she pulled the door open. The next moment Carl's eyes opened wide because his usually dignified mother let out a cry of delight as she exclaimed, "Señor Lummis, where did you—" Her next words were muffled in a huge bear hug as the oddest looking man Carl had ever seen walked in.

The stranger stood back and said, "My dear Juanita,

you look wonderful! *Qua-tzi*, how are you?"

And Carl's mother replied in her native Ácoma Indian tongue. "*Qua-tzi tawa*, I'm well and how are you? So you're back in California at last."

"I had business here in San Francisco so I decided to surprise you and Solomon. It's been many years since we've seen each other."

Without turning around Juana called out, "Carl, I know you're at the top of the stairs listening. Your father's in his study. Go tell him that our good friend Charles Lummis is here."

"Yes, ma'am." Now Carl knew who the stranger was. Running the stairs two at a time, he recalled that last year his parents had received a Christmas card enscribed, "To dear Sol and Juana whom I've known and loved for thirty-seven years. From Charles F. Lummis, December, 1924." Carl's mother had told him that Mr. Lummis was a famous historian and photographer of the Southwest and that each Christmas he sent a card with the same message, changing only the growing number of years that they had all been friends. Then Carl remembered spending a rainy afternoon going through a stack of old magazines in the basement. In one entitled *The Land of Sunshine*, August, 1898, he found an article by Charles Lummis describing a trip to Juana's pueblo of Ácoma in New Mexico. Since Carl's parents had told him little about their early days together and, as yet, he had never visited his mother's tribe, he had read it with great interest. He learned that the Spanish word *pueblo* was used to designate

10

Indian lands belonging to the various tribes of Arizona and New Mexico and that it meant town, village, or the people of any inhabited place. Ácoma, the pueblo where Carl's mother had been born and raised, was known as the oldest, most continuously occupied village in the United States, although how ancient no one knew for sure.

Flinging open the door to his father's study, Carl said, "Papa, Mr. Lummis is here."

"Ach, you don't mean it." Solomon Bibo spoke many languages including fluent Spanish, Ácoma, and Navaho, but when he became excited his English was apt to be tinged with his native German. Throwing his pen on the desk, Solomon swept out of the room calling to Carl, "Come, come, you must talk to Charlie Lummis. There's nobody like him."

"I've sure never seen anybody who looks like him," Carl said.

"Great people can be like that. Ordinary people like you and me, we have to look like everybody else." As Solomon spoke he sped downstairs, his seventy-two years no hindrance. By the time Carl reached the parlor greetings had been exchanged and his father was waving him into the room.

"Charlie, this is Carl. The last of the line, the baby of the family, born eleven years after Leo."

Carl was about to say hello when Solomon in his excitement cut in with "Of course you'll stay here tonight, Charlie. We're having some work done on the house but you can share Carl's room. Would you like to

11

go to Tate's Restaurant or would you rather have supper here, just the four of us?"

"Sol," Mr. Lummis boomed out, "I came to see you and Juana. Let's stay home."

At the supper table Carl had a chance to really study Charles Lummis without being caught. He had been told often enough that it's rude to stare, but in the year 1925 there were not many people walking the streets of San Francisco who resembled this famous man. About five-feet, seven-inches tall, Charles Lummis was slender to the point of skinniness. His white hair hung down to his shoulders and was held back by a red silk bandanna tied around his forehead Indian style. He wore a loose brown corduroy jacket and saggy corduroy pants held up by a Navaho *faja*, a hand-woven band wrapped around his waist instead of a belt. A silver pin engraved with Indian symbols fastened his shirt at the neck and a number of large turquoise rings decorated his fingers. Beaded moccasins completed the outfit.

Carl noticed that Mr. Lummis ate very little and puffed on a big, black cigar between bites. Thin though Mr. Lummis was, Carl admired the whipcord muscles outlined beneath his jacket when he raised his arms in the frequent gestures that punctuated his conversation. Carl remembered his father telling him that Mr. Lummis had covered endless stretches of wilderness on foot, horse, and burro in the United States and South America. It seemed incredible to Carl that this wisp of a man, now in his sixties, ever had the fortitude for such feats.

"And what about Carl?" It was Mr. Lummis speaking.

Carl perked up his ears at mention of his name.

Mr. Lummis gazed at Carl for a moment with eyes the color of a winter sky, but he addressed his questions to Juana. "Has that boy met his relatives on the big rock of Ácoma? Has he snatched off the head of a chicken playing *el gallo* at the Festival of San Juan?"

"Juana and I have had to make business trips to New Mexico in recent years," Solomon explained, "but we have left Carl here, in San Francisco, because we didn't want to interrupt his schooling."

"However," Juana said in her quiet way, "since you are here tonight, Charles, we will tell Carl that, just today, Solomon and I decided that the three of us will drive to New Mexico as soon as school is over and we'll all spend the summer there."

Carl was sent upstairs shortly after dinner since the next day was school and there was homework to be done. Tonight he didn't mind, even though the conversation in the parlor was full of roaring tales of the Old West. The announcement at supper about the proposed summer in New Mexico had meant so much to Carl that he wanted to think about it by himself for a while.

In 1869 Carl's father, Solomon Bibo, had come to the United States from Prussia. He was the third of seven brothers and three sisters who settled in New

Mexico. Solomon started his first trading post at the pueblo of Ácoma in 1882 and it was there that he met and married Juana Valle in 1885. In the next few years he moved his trading post to San Rafael, a little town only a few miles away from the border of the pueblo lands of Ácoma. Carl's four older sisters—Rose, Clara, Celia, and Irma—were born in New Mexico. Leo, Carl's only brother, was born in San Francisco and so was Carl.

At the turn of the century Solomon decided to take his family to California to live because the educational facilities were better. But he retained his sheep ranch and trading post in San Rafael and, later, Carl's older brother Leo had returned to work at the family trading post. The rest of the children had been grown up for many years now and were scattered throughout the West. On the rare occasions when they managed to get together in San Francisco they talked of their childhood in New Mexico and the exciting things they had done. Carl could only listen, having nothing to add since all this had happened before he was born. Once, a couple of years ago, he had blurted out in frustration, "Me and the boy scouts went on a camping trip to Muir Woods and we stayed three days—"

"Forget it, kiddo," Leo interrupted. "Did I ever tell you about the time I started tracking stolen sheep in the middle of a thunderstorm? We rode for days, clean up to Cayenta to Weatherall's ranch—"

"Yes," Carl shouted, "you did tell me, lots of times!"

Worst of all, as Carl had stalked out of the room, he

heard laughter and then the voice of his sister Rosie, saying, "He's only a little boy, Leo. You forget that he's never done any of these things."

Carl turned a page in his algebra book, then realized that he hadn't worked out a single equation on it. He stared at the numbers in front of him and they danced like the legs of a prancing horse. Slamming the book shut, he said aloud, "I can't ride a horse," and he saw himself disgraced in front of his Indian relatives.

"I'll bet they can't play tennis." He enjoyed a brief moment of satisfaction that soured when he faced the fact that he would be the one who had to prove himself and that nobody would be impressed with the cup he had won last week at the High School of Commerce playing in the junior tennis championships. It was a little scary too. He really didn't know any Indians except his mother, and himself and his brothers and sisters who were half Indian.

He sat there, elbows on the desk, running his fingers through his thick black hair. Wrapping his long legs around the back of the chair, he tried to imagine what it would be like on a bucking bronco. Once he had gone to the rodeo at Salinas and he remembered watching a horse they called a killer. The first man who tried to ride him was lucky; he landed in a bale of hay. The second cowboy flew through the air, then smashed across the roof of a hot dog stand and hung there like a broken doll, thin streams of blood trickling down his forehead and into his open, staring eyes.

Would they have horses like that on San Juan's Day at Ácoma? And what was it Mr. Lummis said about snatching off the head of a chicken in the game of *el gallo*?

"I'm tall too," Carl mumbled to himself. "Everybody thinks I'm older than I am. Maybe my Ácoma cousins will name me something like Tall Boy Who Can't Ride a Horse."

Reaching into a secret drawer he had made in his desk, he pulled out the diary he had started to keep a few months ago. He began to write. "Today was the most important day of my life so far. I'm going to New Mexico to spend the summer. There's a man by the name of Charles Lummis—"

"Carl, is your light out?" his mother called from downstairs.

"Yes'm." Stashing the diary away, he switched off the light, and undressed in the dark. It was funny but sometimes when you wanted something a lot and you got it, then you didn't want it anymore. If he stayed here this summer he could hike up to Coit's tower with his friends, play tennis every day, or go to Playland at the beach and ride the roller coaster. Maybe he wouldn't like New Mexico and maybe they wouldn't like him.

Outside the foghorns were blowing their warning on the bay. The sound had a soothing effect and Carl drifted off into uneasy slumber. Suddenly he sat up in bed, wide awake and scared to death. Something was moving around the room silently, furtively, except for the rasp of heavy breathing. Back and forth it went until finally there was the clunk of an object bumping into furniture.

"Damnation!" A penetrating voice rent the air. "You awake, Carl?"

"Oh, it's you, Mr. Lummis," Carl said in relief.

"Sorry to raise such a ruckus but I just split my shins on something that felt like a forty-niner's pickax."

"Why don't you turn on the light? It won't bother me."

"Don't need to. I sleep in my underwear. It saves time going to bed at night and simplifies getting up in the morning."

The bedsprings creaked, then the silence of the night closed in. Carl thought Mr. Lummis had fallen asleep when he heard, "You know something Carl? I envy you."

"Why would you envy me, Mr. Lummis?"

"Because you're going to see it all for the first time. I watched your face tonight when your mother told about the trip. I had a vision of every mesa I'd ever climbed, every burro I'd ever ridden. What an experience you have ahead of you."

"But it's kind of spooky too, Mr. Lummis."

"Sure, it's spooky. That's part of the fun. I was only twenty-six myself when I started writing stories and taking photos of the pueblo tribes back in the eighteen-eighties. It wasn't easy to be accepted. You belong to the Ácomas on your mother's side. You're one of them."

17

"Some people, especially some kids—" Carl paused, then blurted out, "—call me a half-breed."

There was a long silence. Again Carl thought Mr. Lummis had fallen asleep when the booming voice cut through the dark.

"Your father Solomon was born a Jew. Your mother Juana was born an Indian. Your great-grandfather on your mother's side, Martín Valle, was seven times elected governor of the Ácomas. Your grandfather, Isaac Bibo, on your father's side, was a cantor and a learned teacher. Did you know that your father, Solomon Bibo, was also elected governor of the Ácomas? He's the only white man I've ever known to be accorded that honor by an Indian tribe. The office of *gobernador*, or governor, was instituted by the Spanish after the conquest in 1540. The governor stands in relation to the chief much as a prime minister does to a king."

"But Mr. Lummis, how would you feel if you went to the movies with your friends and they showed a serial called *The Santa Fé Trail* and the title of the fourth chapter was 'The Half-breed's Treachery'?" Carl had kept this incident bottled up inside him for over a year now, not mentioning it to anyone, not even his mother and father.

"I'd feel awful," Mr. Lummis said, "just like you did. You can't expect a bunch of stupid fools to produce anything but a bunch of stupid foolishness."

Carl thought about this for a while. As he was about to turn over he heard Mr. Lummis say, "One thing

18

more. There's a mesa, a big table of land called Katzimo, on the pueblo lands of Ácoma. Climb it if you can. I did, long ago, and it was the greatest adventure of my life."

Again there was silence. This time it continued and Carl didn't dare break it. In a few moments it was rent by a snore as penetrating as Charles Lummis' voice.

As Carl pulled the covers up he knew that he was still worried about the new places he was going to see and the new people he was going to meet, but talking to Mr. Lummis had made him more eager than ever to go.

"Mr. Lummis is neat. He says what he really thinks," Carl murmured to himself. Then he fell asleep to the rhythmic alternation of Charles Lummis' snores inside and the blat of the foghorn outside.

2

Carl Meets
His Cousin-Brother

The next few weeks were busy ones for Carl. There were final exams to be taken and that meant studying daily and on weekends besides. In addition he had a secret project that he pursued each night after his light was supposed to be out. After saying good night and pretending sleep for a while, he would steal out of bed, turn on the lamp he had placed on the floor, then he would read the books of Charles F. Lummis. He set himself this task because he knew that Mr. Lummis was an outstanding authority on the Ácomas. This evening he had just found his place when he heard the door open softly and became aware that somebody was standing on the other side of the bed looking down on him.

"Well, Carl, is this the way you sleep at night?" It was his father Solomon. "How long has this been going on and what are you reading?"

In answer to the question Carl handed the book to

his father.

"*Mesa, Cañon and Pueblo*, by Charles F. Lummis. This is his latest, the one he brought us when he was up here recently. I haven't had a chance to read it yet myself. What do you think of it?"

"It's telling me lots of things I never knew before." Though he didn't intend to sound that way there was a note of resentment in Carl's voice.

"So you think we haven't told you enough. Perhaps you're right." Solomon sat down on the edge of the bed. Short, portly, his fair skin showed hardly a line and the lively expression in his gray-blue eyes belied his years. "Your mother and I knew that one day we'd take you to New Mexico. It's not Juana's way to spend time on what she calls useless chatter."

"I didn't mean to criticize."

"This year you'll be bar-mitzvahed into the Jewish faith. That means you assume the duties of a man. A man has the privilege of criticizing." Solomon got up and walked toward the door. "Sometimes I forget that I am more of an age to be your grandfather than your father and that the things I take for granted have never been experienced by you."

The great day was here at last. At five o'clock in the morning Carl was awakened by the raucous screech of the alarm clock next to his bed plus another one going off in his parent's room and yet a third downstairs that had been set as insurance against the failure of the others. Throwing off the blankets, Carl raced down to the kitchen and gleefully throttled the offender. Now, all was silence again but not for long.

"Carlitos, your father wants to pack up the car before we have breakfast. Are your suitcases ready?" Juana was leaning over the balustrade, her black hair falling forward in two wings against her cheeks.

"Mama, let's eat first because the minute the car's packed we'll be impatient to go."

"*Hijo mio*, my son, you'll have to ask your father." In the privacy of her own family Juana often used phrases in Spanish or Ácoma from her childhood at the pueblo. When she and Solomon were married she spoke no English whatsoever nor had she ever been to school because at that time there were no schools on any of the Indian lands in New Mexico. Realizing his wife's desire for education, Solomon sent her to the Carlisle Indian School in Pennsylvania in 1886 where she rapidly picked up the basic skills in English.

Her schooling was interrupted by the birth of her first child, Rose. After that she went ahead on her own, learning while she helped her husband with his business chores. She also actively participated in the innumerable cooking and household chores of a frontier trading post in a primitive country village. Eleven years younger than Solomon, she had the stamina of her ancestors and a quickness of mind that enabled her to make the transition from one world to another with ease.

"All right, Carl." Solomon joined Juana at the head of the stairs. "This is your special vacation so we'll eat first and pack up the car later."

Although the Packard straight-eight was a brand-new, roomy touring car, every inch of space, inside and out, was filled by the time they were ready to go.

As they pulled away from the curb Solomon sang out gaily, "Ladies and gentlemen, we begin our famous tour of the Southwest by driving down historic Market Street in San Francisco, and don't any of you eastern greenhorns call it 'Frisco."

"Papa, how many days will it take us to get to New Mexico?"

"It's a little over a thousand miles. If we're lucky and don't have too many blowouts we'll be there by the fifth day, maybe before. Tomorrow we turn east and follow the National Old Trails highway. About fifteen miles out of Bakersfield we hit dirt roads. Then the fun begins."

Solomon, who had driven the route often, tried to spare them the worst heat of the Mohave Desert by traveling in early morning or late afternoon, but Carl soon discovered that an automobile trip was an endurance contest not an outing. Sand and dust coated his hair, face, and clothes until he was all one color. Although he was thirsty all the time, the radiator drank more of the water they carried with them than he did because, in 1925, the welfare of the car was far more important than that of the people in it. Balloon tires had been available for several years but blowouts were frequent and the repair kit and jack were seldom out of use for long.

On the third day they beat all previous records by having four flat tires, but Solomon, who lost his temper at little things, could be remarkably cheerful under pressure. When they hit a vicious hole, concealed by sand blowing across the road, he held tight to the wheel throughout the explosion, the lurching bump, and the rocking slowdown that followed. Then he said philosophically, "At least it didn't pitch my Stetson out the window the way the last one did. Juana, are you all right? Carl, have you got the repair kit handy?"

The next day the weather improved as they began to climb into the mountains. We're getting close, Carl thought. It made him happy just to think about it because he was so tired of riding.

"I feel like jumping out of the car and running, running, running until I drop in a heap," he announced to no one in particular.

"There is lots of space to run at my pueblo of Ácoma," his mother said. "There are cliff trails and burro trails and haunted trails leading up to the big mesa of Ácoma. There are deep caves where dark gathers at dawn and waits for *oi-shr-tra*, the sun, to go away. There is a great water place, a reservoir carved in the solid rock. When I was a girl I used to go there at first light of day to fill my *tinaja*, my water jug. I would gaze at myself in the clear water, turning my head this way and that to see what I looked like. It was my only mirror. Then when your father came and started the little trading post next to the church on the big rock of Ácoma, I spent much time looking at my

reflection while I brushed my hair with a brush made of yucca fibers. My grandfather, Martín Valle, would call to me, 'Juanita, hurry with my *tinaja*. I am an old man and I am impatient to start the day before my life ends.' I was his favorite granddaughter and to me came the honor of bringing him water each day after my grandmother died and left him alone."

Carl noticed that as they drew closer to Ácoma, his mother spoke more often and at greater length of her life as a girl at the pueblo.

"Tomorrow's the day," Solomon said. "They'll all be waiting there to meet you."

Sometime in the afternoon they would arrive at their destination and Carl's parents decided to drive straight on to Ácoma.

"Your brother Leo is on a buying trip right now, so he won't be at San Rafael. You'll see him later," Solomon said.

The trading post at the nearby town of San Rafael had an adjoining house. Solomon and Juana would headquarter there throughout the summer but Carl would be free to move back and forth between the pueblo of Ácoma and the town of San Rafael. It was his father who proposed this arrangement.

"It's up to Carl," Solomon pointed out. "At times he may want to be at the pueblo. Other times he may want to come to San Rafael, since it's only a few miles from the borders of the pueblo. People are always traveling to the trading post from Ácoma. He can hitch a wagon ride from there or send a message to us at San Rafael and we'll pick him up in the truck."

As the day wore on the countryside grew more and more barren. Even though they were climbing constantly there seemed to be endless desert wastes broken only by huge mesas that looked as though they had just erupted from the floor of the earth. The only softening influence was that the air, especially in the distance, was a palette of hazy lavenders, pinks, and purples.

"Well, Carl, what do you think of it?" Juana asked. "We're close to Ácoma now."

There was a note of pride and suppressed emotion in his mother's voice that made Carl hold back on the unflattering comment he was about to make. Instead he came out with a weak, "It's not like California."

"You can see the beauty of California instantly with your eyes. This country—" Juana hesitated, groping for words "—you feel through your skin and in the beat of your heart. To us, the *hano osach*, the 'children of the sun,' it is a sacred place."

Carl was a little embarrassed at his mother's words and the intensity with which she spoke them. There had always been a steadiness to Juana's temperament. Unlike the volatile Solomon, who could go from one extreme to another in a matter of moments, in Carl's mind his mother was imperturbable. He was beginning to sense another side to her nature. As yet he was not quite at ease with his changing concept.

Solomon took a turn to the right off the main road

and began to follow what seemed to be little more than a pathway.

"Now we are on Ácoma land," Juana said. "In a little while we will see Katzimo, the enchanted mesa, where long ago my people used to live."

"Mr. Lummis climbed Katzimo. I'm going to climb it too," Carl said with assurance.

"Oho!" Solomon exclaimed. "Every boy thinks he wants to climb Katzimo until he sees it. If you do climb it this summer you'll have some adventures of your own to tell Mr. Lummis about. We're going to see him on our way back to San Francisco. He invited us to stay at his home in Pasadena."

They were driving through a vast sandy plain splotched with juniper and coarse grass when suddenly Juana said, "There it is, just ahead of us—Katzimo."

The flatland on which they were traveling was, in itself, a desert some 7,000 feet high in the mountains. Ahead of them rose the great rock table, or mesa, of Katzimo, 431 feet higher, with forty to fifty acres of summit area. Carl remembered reading that this citadel had been the ancient stronghold of the "children of the sun" until, the legend goes, a tremendous flood undermined the natural rock ladder that was the only means of access to the top. All the people had been gathering crops in the valley below except for three women stranded on the summit. Their wails of despair could be heard throughout the valley but, despite heroic efforts, nothing could be done to rescue them. Because of this tragedy the elders decided to relocate on the nearby mesa of Ácoma, not as high as Katzimo at 357 feet but with several areas where an ascent could be made, difficult though it might be.

Centuries later, in 1540, Francisco Coronado was the first Spanish explorer to see the wonders of Ácoma. Coronado left a description of the sky city and the kindly way in which he and his men were received. But later, in 1598, when the Spaniards insisted on submission to the Spanish crown, the people of Ácoma became distrustful. Though they swore obedience to the king of Spain, they had no intention of submitting to any authority other than that of their own tribal chiefs. When Lieutenant Juan de Zaldívar arrived with a small group of soldiers, the Ácoma cacique, Chief Zutucapán, and his war captains, invited the visitors to the summit of the mighty fortress. There the Ácomas fell upon the intruders and in the combat Chief Zutucapán killed Juan de Zaldívar. Five of the Spanish soldiers leaped, in desperation, from the edge of the cliff to the sand below and, miraculously, four of them survived.

As they approached the craggy, formidable mass of Katzimo, Carl understood why it was called the "enchanted" mesa. Exposed by a blazing sun that would have stripped most natural wonders of their mystery, the brooding majesty of Katzimo was only enhanced by the full light of day. Carl remembered his boast of a few minutes ago, that he too would climb Katzimo. Somehow the lordly mesa conveyed the message that he had much to learn before he tried it. He locked the challenge inside himself. One thing he knew, he would not casually mention his ambition again, especially in front of those who had been born and raised here.

To one side of Katzimo and a short distance behind rose a second great mesa almost as tall, upon it the sky city of Ácoma. Carl saw the flat roofs of dwellings on the tableland, the same shade of creamy tan as the straight sides of the rock itself. He watched tiny figures moving about on top, followed the progress of a horse and rider moving swiftly down the side of the mesa. In another area a number of people were descending, gathering at the base of the rock.

"Can we drive all the way to the top?" Carl asked.

"No, there are only burro trails and foot trails," Solomon said. "We have to leave the car at the bottom and walk the rest of the way up."

"They've seen the dust raised by the car," Juana said. "They're coming to meet us."

The eagerness in his mother's voice made Carl's heart beat faster. Details began to stand out in the welcoming party. The older women wore white cotton jumpers and blouses with long sleeves. Over this was a *du-tse-che*, or mantle, of black wool. Pinned to each shoulder was the *oo-ti-natz*, a bright silk scarf that hung down the back. White cotton leggings tucked into moccasins completed the outfit. In contrast, most of the young girls wore modern clothes—cotton dresses or skirts and blouses—looking much the same as the schoolgirls in San Francisco. Both men and boys were dressed in overalls, shirts with patterned neckerchiefs,

30

and the traditional red *banda* worn around the forehead. As they drove the last few hundred yards Carl's eyes were riveted in admiration upon a half dozen stately women walking nonchalantly down a foot trail, balancing on their heads the big *tinajas,* or water jars, that his mother had mentioned before. Carl noticed that the faces in the crowd awaiting them ranged in hue from the coppery tone of his mother and himself to a dark bronze.

Juana leaned out the window, waving her hand and calling. "Plácida, María, *qua-tzi?*"

Now Carl's gaze shifted to a young man who jumped down off a shaggy brown and white pinto pony and ran to join another boy standing with the group. Then Solomon stopped the car, the people swarmed around, and the air was filled with greetings in three languages —English, Spanish, and Ácoma.

An aged gentleman with a red, blue, and white striped blanket draped around his shoulders grasped Solomon's hand and said, "Don Solomona, you are looking well. You do not show the years at all." Later Carl would learn that this honored elder of the tribe was the headman of the oldest medicine society at Ácoma.

"Carlitos, these are my sisters," Juana said, "your Aunt María and Auntie Plácida."

Carl was warmly kissed by both ladies, then asked to turn around for inspection. Plácida exclaimed admiringly, "Juanita, how tall he is, much taller already than Solomon. Taller than his cousins." Plácida motioned to the two young men standing to one side. "Carl, these are your cousins, Wilbert and Horace, and this one—" She paused, searching the crowd with her eyes. "There she is, *sa ma'ak'*, my daughter, your cousin Helen." A shy young girl about twelve years old came forth and shook hands solemnly with Carl.

The three boys looked at each other, then moved awkwardly to one side while the grown-ups exchanged news. The shaggy pony whinnied then pawed the dust, throwing a shower of grit over Carl and his cousins.

"Whose pony is that?" Carl asked.

"He's mine," Wilbert said proudly. "I'll ride him on San Juan's Day in the *gallo* race." Short and stocky, with powerful shoulders, Wilbert's smile was friendly as he patted the pony's flank and whispered to him to calm him down.

"What's his name?" Carl asked.

"His long name is Zutucapán but I call him Zutu."

"I read about Zutucapán. He was a famous chief," Carl said, eager to show his knowledge.

"Zutucapán was our great cacique who beat back the Spanish-Anglos when they tried to conquer Ácoma," Horace said. Unlike Wilbert, Horace was slender and fine-boned, with an abrupt way of expressing himself. His black eyes seemed to be appraising Carl while he spoke. There was no smile, no welcome in his words or manner. Carl's eyes met his and their glances held on neutral ground, neither one accepting nor rejecting the other as yet.

"You going to stay with us at Ácoma tonight?"

Horace asked.

"Yes."

Wilbert mounted his pony and headed for the horse trail that led to the summit of the big rock. "See you later," he called back.

"We don't have radios or electric lights or anything like that up there," Horace volunteered. The cool eyes watched carefully for Carl's reaction.

"That's okay with me."

"How old are you?"

"Thirteen. How about you?"

"The same, but my cousin Wilbert's sixteen. He's strong. He's the best rider in Ácoma and I'm the best runner."

"Does Wilbert live with you?"

Before Horace answered he gave Carl a look that clearly said, it's none of your business, and for a moment Carl wondered if he was going to get a reply. But then Horace seemed to think better of it and his tone was friendly enough as he said, "No, Wilbert lives close by with his mother Aunt María. Some of my family live and work far away from the pueblo now. They came in their wagon a few days ago to take my parents to visit with them this summer. I didn't want to go so I'm staying with Aunt Plácida. That's where you'll be staying."

There was a pause and Carl was about to turn away when suddenly Horace said defiantly, "My great-grandfather, Martín Valle was governor of Ácoma seven times."

"He was my great-grandfather too, and besides, my father, Solomon, was governor of Ácoma."

"I don't believe that. Your father's an Anglo."

"I don't care what you believe, it's the truth. It's easy enough to find out. Ask Aunt Plácida, ask my mom."

"An Anglo should never be allowed to be governor."

"My father was adopted into the tribe when he married my mother."

Their glances were not neutral now. They glared at each other.

"Horace." It was the girl-cousin Helen calling from that pathway that led to the summit of Ácoma. "Come, we are going to eat soon."

The tension was relieved but not dispelled. Carl noticed his parents walking up the foot trail along with members of the welcoming party.

With a quick motion of his hand Horace indicated the path that the group was ascending. "Do you want to walk up the foot trail or do you want to climb the split trail?" He threw the choice at Carl like a challenge.

Without hesitating Carl replied, "The second one, the split trail."

"Follow me." U. S. 1803654

Horace ran swiftly through the piles of talus at the foot of the cliff, weaving his way in and out of the rock fragments which the afternoon sun had baked to oven temperature. Shimmering heat waves assaulted Carl as he stumbled along, trying desperately to keep up. Above him rose perpendicular walls of sandstone indented with curious bits of carving; a fragment of a claw, part of a grotesque profile with an empty eye socket in deep shadow, the wing of a giant bird torn asunder. It was hard to believe that only wind and rain had eroded these forms.

At last Horace stopped. He flung a glance back over his shoulder, then disappeared. When Carl caught up to him he saw a deep cleft in the rock and above him Horace, making his way expertly, with toe and finger holds, up a wall so steep that it seemed impossible to climb.

"I can't do it," Carl said, but even as he thought it he scrambled on, reaching upward for the first indentations, his fingers slippery with sweat, thighs tensed for the push.

"Don't look back," Horace called.

It was a needless warning. To look back would have meant extra motion and Carl knew he did not have an ounce of strength to spare.

About halfway up there was a boulder a few feet square. Horace perched on this for a moment and called down, "Do you want me to wait for you and help you the rest of the way?"

"No." Breathing was difficult now. Showers of sand and dust were dislodged as Horace climbed higher above him. Coughing and sputtering, Carl prayed for strength to reach that boulder where he could rest and catch his breath. At last it was at his fingertips, but as he reached for it his hand struck a sharp edge and a jagged cut in his palm drew a cry that he quickly bit down on. Trembling, he clung to the side of the precipice like a fly as pain shot through him and he watched blood spread out beneath his hand. The hot sandstone absorbed it like a blotter. Now he would try again. Despite the injured hand he got a firm grasp and this time he drew himself up.

Carl sat there for almost five minutes but during that time he did not look down. He bound up his wound as best he could with his pocket handkerchief, inspected the rips in his pants, and closed his smarting eyes, hoping the sudden moisture would wash some of the dust out.

"Need any help?" It was Horace, safe on the rock of Ácoma.

"No." Carl began to climb again. This time it was easier. The cleft had narrowed so that he was able to brace himself by placing his palms on each side. It made the footwork on the slippery sandstone much more secure. It was darker in here but it was a welcome change from the blistering sun.

His legs ached, the muscles in his arms twitched with strain, and the cut in his palm throbbed with the pressure exerted on it against the walls of the cleft. Suddenly the hot sun lashed the top of his head but this time he was glad to feel it. He knew that he was almost there. Pausing for the final exertion, he saw an outstretched hand before him. The skin was bronze, the fingers slender but wiry, curved to match his. Then he heard, "Grab my hand and I'll pull you the rest of the way." Carl didn't know who spoke the words but he was glad of the assistance.

The grip on his slashed palm was tight but he didn't mind. The heave brought him to the top on his feet. He was face to face with Horace.

"You made it," Horace said, and he seemed glad.

"I made it," Carl echoed. "Thanks for pulling me up. I—" But he didn't finish the sentence because suddenly Horace's eyes narrowed, then flicked Carl from head to toe before he turned his back on him.

Confused at the rapid change from friend to stranger, Carl stared at the figure before him. Then he caught sight of Wilbert standing behind Horace, hands on hips, smiling and shaking his head.

"I was sent to look for the two of you," Wilbert said. "Carl, I should have brought you up on my pony Zutu."

"I don't know how to ride a horse," Carl blurted out, relieved at being able to confess his inadequacy to this good-natured relative.

"I'll give you a riding lesson tomorrow. If you can climb the split trail, riding a horse will be as easy as that." Wilbert snapped his fingers. "Horace is the mountain goat in the family. He looks skinny but don't let him fool you. The muscles in his legs are like knots of iron but they work as fast as a *shquwi*, a rattlesnake. You shouldn't have let him talk you into it."

"He didn't. I wanted to try." Carl turned around slowly and looked back down the precipice he had ascended. His head wobbled and he felt a twist of nausea in his middle.

Taking him by the arm, Wilbert said, "Let's go, we'll give you some wild tea to drink. It'll cool you off and push your stomach down your throat, back where it belongs."

"And we'll put some spider plant on that cut. My Aunt Plácida just ground some up fresh today," Horace added, his voice friendly now.

There it was again. One minute Horace held out the olive branch, the next minute he whipped you with it. When Carl got mad, which wasn't often, he stayed that way for a while, but he didn't change in a split second and he wasn't sure that he could get along with somebody who did.

Behind the two boys stretched the three-story stone and adobe houses of Ácoma, built in terraces. The sun dropped in the sky and the big rock and all the buildings on it mellowed to pale pink brushed with lavender shadows.

Wilbert began to walk down the dusty road, then he paused and called back to Carl, "First you better get your face washed before your mother sees you. Come on, cousin-brother."

Carl would learn in the weeks to come that the term "cousin-brother" was a sign of acceptance. He would hear variations of it. A friend who was not related at all, but who was especially close, might be called cousin-friend.

"Hello there, Carl, I've been looking all over for you." It was his father's voice. Carl saw Solomon standing near the church steps waving him on.

As Carl approached, Solomon's glance quickly took in the dirt and dust, the injured hand, the tattered cloth hanging from one trouser leg, but he made no comment. "Have you decided to stay?" he asked.

"Sure."

"Your mother, Leo, and I will be coming to Ácoma to spend San Juan's Day. If you want to come to San Rafael sooner, just tell your Aunt Plácida. She'll get a message to us. If we don't hear, we'll plan on taking you back with us on June 24, the day of the celebration."

"All right, papa." Before running to catch up with his cousins, Carl took a last look at the majesty of Katzimo in the distance. He hoped that the mighty citadel was aware of his existence now.

3

Graveyard of the Ancestors

Carl awoke every few hours to the sound of tinkling bells and some words called out, in the native tongue, over and over. The voice he heard was that of the *kahera*, the town crier, making the rounds of the streets which he did twice during the night and once before dawn. Warmly wrapped in his red blanket against the nip of the mountain air, the *kahera* announced an early summons to the orchards and fields, urging all hands to help with the irrigation and cultivation of the crops that were so important to this farming pueblo. The message was conveyed in a monotone that barely ruffled the edges of the deep slumber into which Carl had fallen as soon as he curled up in his sheepskins on the floor. But in these brief intervals of waking some of the excitement of the day before struggled to the surface.

Just before he went to bed Aunt Plácida had asked him, "Carl, do you know your Indian name and clan?"

"My mother told me a long time ago when I was a little boy. I think it starts something like Kai—" But

41

Carl couldn't remember the rest. "Please tell it to me again."

Aunt Plácida spelled it out for him and Carl wrote down the strange words so he wouldn't forget. During the night this information took the form of a chant that came spontaneously to mind each time he awoke.

> My name is Carl Bibo.
> I belong to *osach*, sun clan.
> My Indian name is Kai-stee-zee.
> It means rainbow.
> Kai-stee-zee
> Rainbow Bibo

By the time Carl had actually stretched himself awake, the morning sun had completed a quarter of its day's journey into the sky. It was very quiet except for a rasping sound coming from across the room. He peered around the sheepskins and saw his cousin Helen bending over a slab of black lava rock on the floor.

"Good morning, Helen. What are you doing?" Carl asked.

"Good morning, Carl. I am rubbing blue corn into meal with my *metate* stone. First my mother rubs it coarse, then I rub it fine. When it is ready we will make *guayave*, paper bread. It is a special food because you are here."

"Where is everybody? It must be late."

"They went to the fields when Pa-yat-ya-ma, sun-father, started his travels through the sky, but my mother said not to wake you."

"I should be helping too."

"Wilbert and Horace will come for you soon. In the meantime, there is your breakfast. Do you like peaches? Those are from our orchards. We cut them and dry them in the sun. Then we keep them in our storeroom all winter. I stewed them up for you. There is goat's milk in the big jug and coffee in the small one. The bread is fresh too. My mother baked a dozen loaves in the oven outside this morning."

Carl dug into the bowl of peaches and after the first tentative sip of goat's milk he poured a generous helping of it over the fruit. He finished by sopping up the juice with several slices of the delicious bread still warm from the oven. While he ate, Helen went silently about her work, not looking up, not speaking again. Her shyness of the day before seemed to have returned.

"Do you go to school?" Carl asked.

"Now is the vacation time but during winter I go to our school in Ácomita," Helen said proudly. "We move off the mesa of Áko where there is no school and move down to our house below at the settlement of Ácomita. My father, Cipriano, is at Ácomita now. He is helping Wilbert's father, Edward, to dig for a well so that he can build a house too for his family to live in when the weather is bad. It makes it easier to go to school. But it is very hard to find water in this land, cousin-brother. Already my father and uncle have been digging for a long time. Whenever they work down

43

eight or ten feet they hit solid rock. But they will do it
before the autumn moons arrive because they do it together, they help one another. That is the way of work
at Áko.

"You call it Áko—"

"The true name of Ácoma is Ákome, which means
'people of the white rock.' When we speak of it among
ourselves we sometimes call it Áko, like you say, for
short."

While he waited for the boys Carl had a chance to
take a good look at his surroundings. Last night he had
been so weary and there had been so many people in
and out that all he had been aware of was the comfort
of warmth, food, and a place to sleep. There were
three main streets running in parallel lines east and
west on the big mesa. The houses on each street were
all connected in a long unbroken line but each dwelling was private with no interior entrance to the others.

The first story of the house had no doorway. This
was the storage room. You climbed an outdoor ladder
to get to the second story, then entered the door of the
room that Carl was in now. In the floor of this living
room was a small trapdoor that was the only entrance
to the storage room below. This kept supplies safe
from animals or intruders and was a relic of the fortress days of centuries past. The third story, used for a
sleeping room by Aunt Plácida and Helen, was
reached by tiny outdoor steps. The first and second
stories were terraced, forming ample porch space. It
was a practical and secure arrangement.

44

Carl was sitting on a wooden bench that ran along one wall of the living room. During the day this bench was comfortably padded by the sheepskins and Navaho blankets used for sleeping at night. In a kind of informal division of labor, different tribes specialized in a particular article which they traded to one another or sold commercially. The Navahos were famous for rugs and blankets, the Ácomas for pottery, the Zuñi for baskets.

There were several windows in the room but instead of glass, large sheets of translucent gypsum, found naturally in the rock on Ácoma land, were used to allow light to come through. In one corner was a small adobe fireplace. Beside it, on the wall, hung strings of parched chile peppers and a *tasajo*, a twist, of dried melon. On the opposite wall a number of heavy silver and turquoise necklaces were hung on pegs along with buckskins and *oo-ti-natz* intricately woven in bright colors. These were special clothes worn only on ceremonial occasions.

Next came a *santo*, or saint, in a glass case, and Carl knew from his reading that it was Father Juan Ramirez in 1628 who, through his unselfish devotion, had converted the Ácomas to the Catholic religion. But the aged priest had been long gone from Ácoma by the time the great pueblo revolt of 1680 took place. Many tribes were involved in this successful overthrow of the Spaniards led by an Indian named Popé from the pueblo of San Juan. The pueblos most directly involved were northern tribes located near the city of Santa Fé, but Ácoma was in full sympathy with ousting the conquerors. The pueblo nations remained independent until 1699 when the Spanish subdued them again. Although the pueblo inhabitants continued after that to be baptized as Catholics, they also practiced their ancient tribal rituals. Ever since, the two faiths had lived compatibly together and, though there had not been a resident priest at Ácoma for many years, a visiting Father conducted services for certain festivals and other important occasions.

Carl had completed his inspection of the room and saw that everything was very clean and orderly. He was suddenly ashamed of his open suitcase on the floor —shirts, shoes, and papers spilling out of it in all directions. He had just knelt down and started to stuff back some of its contents when he heard a whistle outside.

"That's Wilbert," Helen said, "come to take you for a riding lesson."

Carl sprang to his feet, the suitcase forgotten. As he ran to the door he called back, "Good-bye, Helen."

"*Tru-shotts*," Helen said.

Pausing for a moment, Carl said, "*Tru-shotts*?"

"That means good-bye in our language."

"Oh. Well, then *tru-shotts*, cousin-sister."

He was rewarded by a smile of approval as Helen bent once more over her grinding stone.

Carl was glad it was Wilbert who had volunteered to teach him how to ride a horse and not Horace. When he climbed awkwardly into the saddle, on the plains below the big mesa of Ácoma, Wilbert smiled encouragement.

"Don't worry if you feel clumsy as a *kuwhaia*, a bear, cousin-brother," Wilbert said. "The idea is to crawl up there any way you can and stay on."

At first Wilbert led Zutu along slowly. Carl felt like a kid taking a pony ride at the amusement park but after a while he forgot about everything except learning how. When Wilbert gave him the reins he went along for a ways at the same leisurely pace, then Wilbert asked, "Do you want to go faster?"

"Faster, but not too fast," Carl replied.

Wilbert said something in Ácoma to Zutu and Zutu began to trot. Carl started laughing because he was bouncing up and down like a tennis ball. Soon Wilbert got to laughing too, and then Horace, who had come along later to watch the lesson. But Horace was laughing like he was glad that Carl looked silly.

All of a sudden Zutu took off and Carl heard Wilbert shouting, "Hold tight with your knees! Don't grab the saddle."

About the time Carl was sure he couldn't stay on a minute longer Zutu slowed down and stopped to nibble at a clump of grass. Wilbert had told Carl that Zutu sometimes liked to play games with people but that he was never mean. Carl rode a while longer and that was the end of the first try. It hadn't been nearly as bad as Carl imagined it would be. Wilbert said they'd do it again tomorrow. Carl noticed that Horace had left by the time the lesson was over.

The next day Carl rode around for almost an hour,

gaining confidence as he learned to relax. Horace had appeared again, standing in the background, not saying anything as he watched Carl's progress.

"I think I'd like to try a gallop," Carl called to Wilbert.

Wilbert called back, "You sure you want to?"

"I've got to try it sometime, don't I?" Carl said.

"Okay, but remember what I told you yesterday. Grab tight with your knees but don't grab the saddle horn, and talk to him, explain what you want. Horses like to be talked to, especially Zutu."

They started off easy. The floor of the valley was level, and way off to his left Carl could see a pastor, a shepherd, and a herd of sheep like blobs of cotton candy, moving along with a big yellow-haired dog running back and forth yipping. Carl began to think, there's nothing to this. I guess I'm a natural.

"Come on, Zutu, let's give it a go," he said out loud, pressing his knees in tight. And did that pony go! It reminded Carl of the movies when they speed up the reel and everything goes zip, zip, zip. The sheep got closer and closer, the shepherd turned around and tugged at the red *banda* on his forehead, the dog ran in circles barking like crazy.

"Stop, Zutu, stop!" Carl yelled, and Zutu stopped. How that horse put on the brakes! Carl hung on with all his might but Zutu didn't stay stopped because, just then, Carl heard Horace calling,

"*How-eh-ima*, Zutu!"

Zutu made a funny snort like a horselaugh and

48

started up again with a jerk. That's when Carl flew off him backwards. He knew that Horace had meant him to do just that. Carl landed sitting up in the dirt, shaken, but all in one piece. Then he watched in amazement as Zutu came trotting over with his ears pointed forward, making little nickering sounds and generally acting like he'd done Carl some kind of favor. Wilbert had told him that this was the way Zutu behaved when he was pleased with himself. Carl could see Wilbert and Horace running toward him in the distance and he knew he had to get up and ride Zutu again, right away. By the time the boys reached him he was back in the saddle.

"You did right," Wilbert called. "The first time you get tossed you have to jump on quick and ride again."

Looking straight at Horace, Carl said, "I wouldn't have gotten thrown except that Horace called '*How-eh-ima*, Zutu.' Horace doesn't think I know what that means, but I do. It means, 'Come here, Zutu.'"

Horace looked right back and said defiantly, "I was only trying to help."

"Thanks for nothing. I can do without that kind of help."

They were glaring at each other now. Horace clenched his fists and took a step forward. Carl began to climb out of the saddle when Wilbert walked quickly between the two boys. Taking the reins, he turned Zutu around fast, heading him back toward Ácoma. The sudden move sat Carl down hard on the horse. Wilbert immediately began leading Zutu away from

49

Horace as he said with a laugh, "Well, Carl, you aren't exactly ready to be a rider in the *gallo* race on San Juan's Day next week but all you need is practice. You learn real good."

By the end of the week Carl had become acquainted with the *kahera*'s routine. He knew that the third time the town crier came around it was getting close to dawn. The first few days he had been so tired from exercise and the unaccustomed altitude that he hadn't given a thought to the diary he had promised himself to keep. This morning he made a secret pledge to get up shortly after the *kahera*'s last round, steal out on the rooftop of the house, and scribble down all he could remember.

Shortly after he awoke to the tinkling bells, he slid the diary and pencil out from under the sheepskins, reached for the sweater he had laid out for the purpose and, in his bare feet, eased out the door and onto the roof. The chill mountain air snapped him wide awake. Pulling the sweater over his head, he looked up at the silver disc of a full moon and a night so sprinkled with stars that it seemed as though the lights of a big city had been flung into the sky. The outlines of the buildings of Ácoma were bleached skeletons. Not a tree, nor a flower grew on this fortress where every drop of water was needed for the necessities of life. At this hour, with streets empty of people and drained of color, Ácoma looked timeless and indestructible.

A slight movement across the street caught Carl's

eye. A black and tan dog ambled out of the shadows, cast a curious glance at Carl, then went on his way, tail wagging ever so slightly. Heaving a sigh of relief that the animal hadn't barked everybody awake, Carl seated himself cross-legged, then opened the diary and began to write as best he could in the semidark.

By the time Carl closed the diary and stuffed it into his pocket, the stars were beginning to fade and the raucous crow of a rooster made it official that dawn was on the way. On a sudden impulse Carl climbed down the ladder that led to the street. He began to walk toward the church, scuffing his bare feet in the dust. The houses turned from gray-white to pale cream and he hurried along, wanting to reach the graveyard so he could see mighty Katzimo take shape in the distance when the first fingers of light stroked the dark away.

Rounding the corner of the church, he ran a little way, then stopped. A man of the tribe was standing there facing the east. He was completely motionless and very straight, arms folded beneath his blanket. Even though Carl was barefoot there had been a clatter of stones and a dust cloud stirred up by his running, so he knew the man was aware of him. But not by so much as a twitch of the cheek did the gentleman recognize the presence of another person. Not knowing what to do, Carl stood motionless too, and though he was embarrassed, he soon lost all thought of himself in contemplation of the dawn and the emergence of Katzimo.

At first, the great rock looked like a watery mirage such as he had seen in the Mohave Desert. But instead of receding, it grew with the growing light, adding depth, breadth, and stature, filling all of Carl's sight until it became a reddish swirling mass. He closed his eyes, momentarily blinded, feeling as though he had looked directly into the sun for too long a period of time. When he opened his eyes Katzimo had settled into its daytime majesty; aloof, impregnable and, this morning, very remote.

Suddenly the man turned. "You are Carl Bibo," he said. He had the deep chest and broad shoulders of the mountain Indian. His eyes were very black and keen, but streaks of gray in his long dark hair showed him to be past middle age.

"Yes, sir."

"I am called Lorenao Watshm Pino. You are out early, my son."

"I wanted to watch Katzimo in the dawn. Is that what you were doing?"

"At this time of year I come out at first light to watch sun-father rise over that mesa, far away where the sky meets the earth." Lorenao Watshm Pino pointed to the spot then moved his finger to another position. "When sun-father has almost reached that place in the north then I can tell the day that he will turn south. You call this the summer solstice. We call it *di-dya-micoko*."

"Do you know my mother, Juana, and my father, Solomon?"

"I do. They were married in the church right behind you. Have you seen it yet?"

"No. My cousins haven't taken me."

"I will take you. But first I will show you where your ancestors are buried here in the graveyard in front of the church. Come along."

Though Carl had seen few graveyards, he realized that this one was unique. To begin with there were none of the softening influences of green lawns, floral displays, and tall, leafy trees. The enormous plot was stark, the dusty adobe soil broken only by wooden crosses and headstones. Here and there a sprinkle of coarse grass was already drying up in the heat of the summer sun. The graveyard was enclosed on three sides by an adobe wall. Every few feet, on top of the wall, there were strange heads molded of the same material. Most of the faces had bits of glass or stone for eyes. The expressions were not grotesque—some were smiling, many seemed to have been sculpted in a spirit of humor. Carl had expected to be afraid of these guardians of the dead but instead he felt at ease with them.

"Your *ba-ba* and *na-na* are buried here. Your grandmother and grandfather."

Carl stopped, filled with a sense of awe. He had never seen a grave before that belonged to him. His father's family was buried far off in Europe. It was the first time that death had become a reality. He could feel the scrutiny of Lorenao Watshm Pino and he felt suddenly shy and yet very honored that this dignified elder had taken him on this personal tour.

Carl noticed that several of the graves had pieces of pottery scattered over the mounds. He wanted to ask why, but hesitated for fear he might be prying. The sharp eyes of Lorenao Watshm Pino saw the direction of his gaze and he explained.

"Those are the newly dead. After burial a ceremonial bowl of water is broken over the grave to give the departed his last drink. It is our custom. Do you know that it took forty years to make this graveyard? First, the Ácoma workers made a frame of stone walls at the edge of the mesa that is forty feet deep. Then they hauled up dirt from the far plain, in sacks made of buffalo hide, to fill this big box two hundred feet square. The timbers of the church were brought from Mount San Mateo twenty miles away. Even the earth to build the houses of Ácoma had to be hauled because all this . . ."—Watshm Pino paused and made a sweeping gesture that included the whole sky city on the mesa—". . . was only bare rock. It was not done by the labor of horses. It was not done by the labor of burros. It was carried on the backs of men."

"But why didn't they use horses?" Carl asked.

"Before the Spanish-Anglos came in 1539 there were no horses and no burros. For a long time after, there was no trail that a horse could climb."

As Watshm Pino spoke, he turned in the direction of the church. Carl followed him up the broad stone steps and through the simple doors painted white and pink. As soon as he entered Carl felt the permanent chill that came from ten-foot-thick adobe walls. The ceiling, sixty feet high, was beamed by hand-carved timbers aged to a rich walnut brown, a contrast to whitewashed walls. There were no seats and few decorations aside from a gaily colored mural behind the altar depicting various saints.

"Your mother and father were married here on May 1, 1885. It was then that your father was adopted as a member of the tribe."

"Were you here too?" Carl asked.

"All of the pueblo was here. I was a young boy but I remember well. First they were married in the nearby town of Cubero, just outside the boundaries of Ácoma, by a Justice of the Peace. Then they were married again, here in this church, by Father Juillard."

"Was my father governor of Ácoma then?"

"No, but shortly after that I remember him carrying the Lincoln cane, and only the governor does that."

"What is the Lincoln cane?"

"In the year 1863 the governors of seven pueblos went to Washington to see Father Abraham Lincoln. They had much talk with this great president about the boundaries of our land grants. When all talk was finished, President Lincoln gave to each governor a silver-headed cane. It is written on the cane: A. Lincoln, Prst., U.S.A., Ácoma, 1863. When the governor of our pueblo is elected each year in January, this cane is passed on to him."

"Where did my father have his trading post?"

Lorenao Watshm Pino walked through a side door of the church, motioning Carl to come along. Carl followed him down a covered walkway that ran along the side of a patio built in Spanish style. The garden was a dreary ruin in the morning light. A few decayed stumps of trees and snaggles of dried-up bushes were the only reminders that here Franciscan Fathers, in centuries past, had lived and struggled to re-create a bit of Spain on the arid unyielding ground.

Watshm Pino climbed a narrow winding staircase, then walked out on a porch above the cloister that was built upon its corner. This covered balcony, with its hand-carved beams and railings, was open on two sides. It commanded a sweeping view of the pueblo of Ácoma.

"The first trading post of your father was here. He carried only a few things because he had not many supplies when he started out as a young man, nor is there much space to store them here. When he prospered he moved to a bigger store away from the pueblo. And now, Carl Bibo, I must leave."

"Thank you for telling me all these things. Thank you for—"

But Lorenao Watshm Pino was gone. Carl hung over the balcony railing and watched his progress through the streets. Walking rapidly, Watshm Pino headed straight for one of the adobe houses and climbed a ladder that, unlike the others in the pueblo, was ornamented with strange symbols. Carl could see several gray-haired men emerge from the doorway of the house to greet him, then they all disappeared inside. There were people in the streets now and the sounds of the working day brought Carl back to the present and made him aware that he wanted breakfast.

"Why were you talking to *ga-tsi*, the cacique?"

Carl turned around quickly at the sound of Horace's voice. "His name is Lorenao Watshm Pino. He showed me the church. What's it to you, anyway?"

"Watshm Pino is his Anglo name. He is *ga-tsi*, the chief of the tribe."

"He didn't tell me that. Does he belong to our clan, Horace, the sun clan?"

"No, the chief always has to be of the antelope clan. It is Ácoma tradition."

"But he knew who I was."

"It is the business of the chief to know everything," Horace said abruptly. "Why were you out so early? Aunt Plácida sent me to look for you."

"I don't know. I woke up. I was restless." Carl was surprised that Horace had turned up at home long enough to be sent on an errand. Expecting to see Horace often at the house, Carl scarcely caught a glimpse of him except at supper when Horace ate fast and departed long before the rest of them were finished. He was never around at breakfast and had an uncanny way of timing himself so that he was sleeping when Carl went to bed, or he did not come in until after Carl had dozed off.

One evening Aunt Plácida had said to him jokingly, "Horace, you remind me of a *shask*, a road runner,

58

startled by a hunter. You are always scurrying away."
Horace had answered lamely, "I go down to the fields
to help with the work as often as I can." But Carl knew
this wasn't true. He had seen Horace in the distance
several times, walking aimlessly and usually alone. It
was obvious that Horace was trying to avoid him. Carl
wouldn't have cared if he could have been with Wilbert more, but Wilbert was enough older so that his
duties were different and often kept him away.

I'll keep trying to make friends for a while anyway,
Carl thought. Maybe if I show him how really interested I am in Ácoma we'll get along better. Moving
over at the railing, Carl made room so that Horace
could join him. "Look, Horace, see that house over
there, the one with the funny ladder with the designs
on top? That's where the cacique went when he left.
Why does it have a ladder different from the rest?"

"That is the *estufa*, the sacred chamber, named by
our people Mauharots. It is the meeting place of the
cacique, the war chiefs, their lieutenants, and the
cheani or medicine men. They are all there this morning."

"What do they do when they meet?" Carl asked.

"Now they prepare for the day of *di-dya-micoko*."

"The summer solstice," Carl said, remembering
what Lorenao Watshm Pino had told him that morning.

Horace's eyes flicked over Carl as he said, "You
know too many things, cousin Carl." His tone hard-
ened in that swift change from friend to foe that still

59

surprised Carl each time it happened.

Immediately on the defensive, Carl muttered, "I know what I was told by the chief. You got any objections to that?"

Then Horace said, "Look down in the square."

Reluctantly, because Horace made it sound like an order, Carl looked down at the big plaza below.

"If somebody steals," Horace said, "or gets drunk, or breaks a law of the tribe, or asks too many questions like you did, the *pregón*, the herald, calls all the people to the plaza. Then the governor shouts from the housetop and tells the whole pueblo what bad act has been done. The *alguaciles*, the sheriffs, come with big rawhide whips. They tear off the shirt and lash the back of the guilty one until blood runs. So be careful, cousin."

"Horace, you know that nobody has been whipped for many years. We have a court now."

Carl whirled around when he recognized Wilbert's voice.

Wilbert's expression was as pleasant as ever but, looking straight at Horace, he said, "People can be punished for not telling the truth too."

"I wasn't lying," Horace said.

"But you weren't telling all of the truth," Wilbert insisted.

Without saying another word Horace brushed past Wilbert and Carl and ran down the stairs.

"Come along and eat your breakfast, Carl," Wilbert said. "You're going to help us in the fields this morning, then, this afternoon, you and Horace are going to practice for the races on San Juan's Day."

"Me?" Halfway to the stairs, Carl stopped in surprise. "But you said I couldn't ride a horse well enough to—"

"You can't, but you can run. There are two *gallo* races. One is on foot, the other on horseback. The young boys run by age group in the foot race, way down to three-year-olds and way up to boys the same age as you and Horace."

"Oh." Carl hurried down the worn stairs. He didn't want Wilbert to read the expression on his face.

Wilbert followed behind explaining further details as they went along. "Your mother and father and other relatives will come and Mexican-Anglos from San Rafael. Lots of Anglos will come from other states too. Almost everybody in the world comes to see the races. Navaho tribesmen, Zuñi, Lagunas . . ."

Carl walked faster through the streets of Ácoma. He and Horace were the same age. They would be competing against each other. Horace had been in these races all his life. It was brand-new to Carl. Everybody would be watching.

"Whoa there, Carl," Wilbert shouted. "You're not running the race yet. Slow down. I can hardly keep up with you. You must be real hungry."

4

If You Lose, You Win

"Wake up, Carl, wake up. We must all go to church. On San Juan's Day the Father comes to say Mass."

Carl blinked his eyes open and for a moment he wondered who the strange girl was. Then he said, "Helen, you look really nice."

Today, instead of her usual modern dress, Helen was wearing spotless white buckskin *botas*, or leggings, and white beaded moccasins. Her black *du-tse-che* was fastened with big silver pins and several strings of turquoise beads around her neck lent a brilliant touch of color. The *oo-ti-natz* hanging from her shoulders was of finest silk woven in an elaborate pattern of peacock blue and coral red.

"Thank you, cousin Carl," Helen said primly. "I wear my ceremonial clothes for the dance. We celebrate two things today—San Juan and *di-dya-micoko*. You must wear your best clothes too."

Carl grabbed a towel and headed for the cistern on the north side of the village. This was a deep natural hollow filled with rainwater where laundry and bodies were washed. The big reservoir on the south mesa was used solely as a drinking supply. As he fitted his bare feet into the indentations in the rock pathway, worn by Ácomans over hundreds of years, Carl made up his mind that he would do his best in the foot race today, but no matter what happened he would not get angry at Horace. A few days back Wilbert had given him some oblique advice. "San Juan's Day is for fun, cousin Carl. The *gallo* race is only a game. All must play it happy. To lose your temper is what we call bad medicine, but you call it bad—bad . . ."

"Sportsmanship," Carl supplied.

"That's the word."

At the time Carl had wanted to say, you'd better tell that to Horace too, but he knew that Wilbert had acted in friendship. Besides, it could be that Wilbert had also taken Horace aside and told him the same thing.

There was nobody else at the cistern and Carl knew that the hour was growing late. Stripping to the waist, he lathered himself with soap made from the yucca plant, then rinsed with dippers of water poured from an olla, a clay jug, that he had brought along for the purpose. The contact with the icy water prodded him along fast with his morning bath.

While he finished toweling himself dry he climbed back up the path, not wanting to waste time. But when he got to the top he paused. He could just see a part of Katzimo off to one side. No matter where he went, no matter what he was doing, he was always conscious of the mighty mesa. He no longer told himself that he would climb Katzimo before the summer ended. He knew it was not as simple as that, but the desire was stronger than ever.

Carl was about to head for home when a strong gust of wind blew something through the air that fell on the path behind him. The wind often came up very suddenly at Ácoma, driving through the streets, lashing the cheeks with sand, blinding the eyes with dust. Carl retraced his steps halfway down to the cistern and the moment he saw the object he knew what it was. Picking it up, he stood there turning it over in his hand. It was a piece of cedar wood about as long as a pencil and twice as thick. Carved in the shape of an arrow, there were feathers tied around the pointed end.

Several days ago, on the eve of the summer solstice, he had noticed some of his relatives carving these sticks in different designs, then tying them in bunches of four and wrapping them in corn husks. Before dawn someone had knocked on the door and he heard one of the family whisper when he opened it.

"Here are the *hachamoni*, the prayer sticks, to offer to sun-father."

Glancing up, Carl saw, off to one side and out of reach, a stone shelf covered with dozens of prayer sticks. It was impossible to reach this ledge from where he stood. Wanting to put it back where it belonged, he ran up the path and dropped the stick onto the ledge

64

from above. As he did this he said aloud, "May I do all right in the *gallo* race. May I climb Katzimo this summer."

Carl and his cousins joined the rest of the people pouring out of the houses, urged along by the clanging of the church bell. As they neared the plaza Helen pointed out the north tower of the church and the muscular young man inside it. Cobblestone in hand, this boy beat with all his might on the old bell brought over from Spain, varying the rhythm from fast to slow, obviously enjoying his work.

"It is called the Church of San Estevan, or St. Stephen," Helen explained, "but the inscription on the bell reads San Pedro, 1710. No one knows why the patron saint of Ácoma was changed at one time and then changed back. Look, Carl, there's Aunt Juana, Uncle Solomon, and your brother Leo. They've come to join us."

For a few seconds Carl felt like a stranger looking at other strangers. He was startled to realize how completely he had been absorbed into the life around him in the past few weeks. Then his mother caught sight of him and when she smiled and waved he began to walk faster. It was almost a run but not quite because it wouldn't have been proper in front of the church and, besides, it wouldn't have been dignified.

Beaming at her son, Juana said, "Carlitos, *hijo mio,* you look different."

"I think he's grown an inch," Solomon said.

"Hey, buddy, don't you have a word for me?" Carl's brother Leo cuffed him lightly on the shoulder, then shook hands with an iron grip. Short and stocky like Solomon, Leo was a voluble outgoing young man to whom inactivity was the worst torture in the world. Solomon and Juana had found it almost impossible to keep Leo in school long enough to comply with state rules. At a certain point they gave up and let him work off his energies at the trading post as well as helping with the sheep business that Solomon shared with his brothers. As long as Leo was in action—counting lambs, weighing wool, hiring men, or racing his rebuilt Model T Ford in Albuquerque—he was happy.

"Bet you don't know what I'm going to do today," Carl said to his brother.

"Bet I don't. I'm all ears. Tell me."

"I'm going to be in the *gallo* race—the foot race, I mean."

"Go on, you're kidding."

"Were you ever in it?" Carl asked anxiously.

"Never."

Carl smiled. At last he was doing something Leo had never done.

The crowd was filing into the church and Aunt Plácida motioned to the family to come along. The worshipers stood solemnly throughout the entire ceremony. Even the smallest children displayed the patience and control instilled in them from birth.

The minute the service ended there was a *pom pom pom* outside in the square as a resonant *tombé*, or drum, began a broken beat accompanied by the sharp spat of revolvers fired into the air. The festivities of San Juan's Day were officially underway. Carl felt a surge of excitement mixed with a shiver of apprehension now that the race was almost upon him. Behind him he heard the piercing wail of the official chanters, a chorus composed mostly of older men.

"Carl." He looked up at the sound of his name but didn't recognize the awesome figure coming toward him. The young man was nude to the waist, his body painted a vibrant blue-green. His long hair swung black and shiny in the sun and multicolored parrot feathers were fastened to the crown of his head. He wore a kilt, or skirt, with fox skins hanging down the back, and fastened just below his knees were little silver bells. His moccasins were topped with fur.

"It's me, Wilbert. I'm one of the dancers. Listen, Carl, I just wanted to tell you that you don't have to be in the *gallo* race if you don't want to. I pushed you into it and maybe I shouldn't have. So long, they're calling us. I don't want to be late."

Carl caught his cousin by the arm. "Wait a minute. I want to be in the race. I don't know why, but I do."

"Okay." Wilbert sped off to the other side of the street where a group was assembling.

Carl stood there watching the dancers but he was not thinking of the impressive spectacle before him. Somehow Wilbert's last-minute reprieve had taken away the hollow feeling of wishing he could stand to one side and watch the celebration like any

68

other spectator.

Across the plaza, on the second story of one of the houses, Carl saw a familiar figure jumping up and down, waving a red *banda*. Even through the noise of the dance he heard his name called. It was Horace.

Carl began to weave his way around the spectators. Boys of all ages detached themselves from their families, heading in the same direction, gathering for the foot race, the next event after the dance. Behind him the thump of the *tombé* grew stronger and faster as the dancers moved in precise and patterned steps. Suddenly Horace appeared at his side, handing him the little switch with which he would try to strike the rooster, *el gallo*.

"Come on with me, Carl. We're in back because we're almost the biggest."

The line was forming now. It started up front with the little boys, each one clutching his rooster switch. In the big plaza the dancers were leaving. Two young men carrying poles, from which a live rooster was suspended on the cord between them, moved into the open space. The object of the game was for each contestant, in turn, to reach up with his switch and strike at the rooster until the time when some particularly adventurous boy was able to jump high enough to free it. He would then make off with the bird, running as fast as he could through the streets, pursued by all the others, who would try to wrest it from him. People of Spanish descent as well as Indians throughout New Mexico played some form of this game, usually on horseback. No one knew its origins for sure. It was similar to medieval contests held by knights in Europe centuries before.

It was not the race itself that bothered Carl. It was the violent death of the rooster that made him queasy. He had been told that inevitably, in the heat of the contest, the rooster was torn to bits as one after another struggled with the squawking fowl until, at the end, only bloody bits were left. The later contest would be the same, only that time the participants would be on horseback, which lent additional excitement and danger.

Carl took his place in the line directly behind Horace. The *tombé* began its bass boom and the *alguacil*, the sheriff, moved forward with both hands raised, palms out, to silence the crowd.

"*Hai-ko*," shouted the *alguacil*.

At this signal the small boys started forward in the high-stepping semi-hop that was maintained by all contestants until the moment when someone snatched the rooster.

Carl watched the little fellows switch the air as the rooster flapped his wings in the struggle to free himself from the cord that bound him. The voluble crowd kept up a running stream of comments as each contestant made his try. The line was moving along now and a nine-year-old managed to dislodge a single feather which brought a loud shout of "*Olé, que macho el joven!* Hurray, what a man that boy is!" from a group of Mexicans standing near the pole. Dressed in white ruffled shirts and tight black pants with silver embroidery down the legs, the splendor of their outfits among the spectators was rivaled only by the Navahos on the other side. These men wore loose velveteen blouses with belts of enormous silver discs that gleamed in the fierce summer sun. Around their necks were layers upon layers of elaborate turquoise jewelry, hand-fashioned and worth a small fortune.

It was just as Wilbert had said—everybody in the world was here and everybody was watching. The line moved forward. As Carl watched the efforts of those ahead he knew that he had a chance to capture the rooster on the very first try. He was taller than anyone else in the contest except for the last boy directly behind him. But did he want to? A plan began to form in his mind which might enable him to acquit himself with honor but without having to participate in the dismemberment of the unfortunate bird.

There was only one boy ahead of Horace now and for a split second he actually had his fingers on the leg of the rooster, drawing an *"Ei-yei nashdui!* Oh, you wildcat!" from the excited Navahos.

Then Horace stepped forward. He took a tremendous switch at the rooster with one hand and grabbed high with the other, getting a hold around the neck of the bird. But the frantic rooster slashed out with his beak at the same time that Horace grasped him. Horace was forced to let go to avoid more wounds, while blood ran down his arm.

With his last hopping step, Carl suddenly tossed the

switch away, then, jumping with all his might, he flung both arms high. Tugging on the cord with his left hand he fastened his right firmly around the bird's neck. As he came down he stumbled and the crowd breathed out a tremendous *"Cuidado!* Be careful!"

With the wisdom of the doomed, the rooster tried to flap its way out of his grasp and managed to free one wing before Carl regained his footing and started running down the dusty street. Boys followed after him, every which way, sorting themselves out rapidly as the small ones got left behind and the older and stronger ones gained speed.

As he sped past the church and across the uneven rock trail that led to the south mesa, he wished with all his might that he could let the rooster go. But this would not be playing the game according to the rules. He heard footsteps behind him and knew that a number of older boys were gaining on him. He was far from being the fastest in the group. It was inevitable that some of them would overtake him, but this fitted into his plan.

He tried harder, giving it everything he had. Here on the south mesa there were no dwellings. The bare rock was slippery and irregular, especially around the area that enclosed the reservoir used for drinking water. By taking this route Carl suddenly realized that he had trapped himself because the only way out was back the way he had come. That narrow trail was now filling with his pursuers. He heard the slap of moccasined feet closing in behind him, then he lost the sound as he gasped for breath and his ears rang with the pounding of his own heart.

Throughout the run the rooster had never stopped struggling. Carl felt his hand grow slippery around the bird. Pausing for an instant to get a firmer clutch he saw fingers reach out and felt a tug on the tail feathers. Whirling around he looked into the face of the tall boy who had been behind him in the line-up for the race. Bending over, Carl enfolded the squawking fowl in both arms, clutching him tight, praying for a few seconds' grace. As he did, he caught sight of Horace running on the slick rocks along the edge of the reservoir with the swiftness of an antelope.

Although Carl and his opponent were almost the same height, the other boy was a good twenty pounds heavier. Carl felt arms like steel encircle his body and though he kept his hold on the rooster he knew his feet were going out from under him as the boy tried to wrestle him to the ground.

"*Mutietsa*, boy, give it up," the other said with a good-natured laugh.

Carl had no breath to waste on words. Blinded by perspiration, he closed his eyes and held on. His feet slipped, heels dragging on the ground as the boy tugged him backward.

"You're going over the side into the reservoir!"

"No, he's not," someone cried out.

The boy let go and with the sudden release Carl crashed to the ground and rolled over, still clutching the bird. Horace had made a flying tackle, shoving

Carl's opponent to one side.

"Here, Horace, take him, he's yours," Carl shouted. "I can't hold him a minute longer."

The bird was transferred before the big boy was on his feet, and Horace ran off with him around the other side of the reservoir. By now all the pursuers had been sucked down into the area where the struggle had taken place. The path back into the town was clear except for a few smaller lads who offered no competition to the sure-footed Horace. Carl sat where he had fallen, wiping his forehead with the sleeve of his shirt, gulping air as he tried to catch his breath. Like a magnet, Horace had drawn all the others back up the trail in pursuit. Even the stragglers had reversed direction to follow the leader.

Completely alone now, Carl looked longingly at the forbidden water supply, wishing he could immerse his whole aching body in its cool, green depths. Lacking any kind of drinking vessel, he hesitated to pollute it by dipping his dirty hands in it. He got up slowly, dusting off his trousers, picking feathers from the front of his shirt. He had done what he had to do, but he would leave the rest of the contest to the others, including the fate of the rooster.

"Hey, Carl, what are you doing down there?" Leo walked down the pathway to the reservoir. "The horse race is about to begin. You don't want to miss that. It's wild."

"All right, I'm coming but I've got to get a drink of water. I'm dry as a bone."

As Leo approached, he held something out. "I brought a bottle of soda pop down for you. I figured you'd need it after that race. You did great."

"How did Horace make out?"

"Terrific! He ran them all ragged up and down the streets and right off the mesa. They never did get the whole bird away from him. He finally gave the scraps that were left to one of the little kids. Between you and Horace, you guys really kept it in the family."

"That's the way I planned it," Carl murmured.

"What did you say?"

"Listen, Leo, do you know what a prayer stick is?"

"Sure."

"Do you think they work?"

Leo looked at him for a long minute. "The half of me that's Indian knows they work."

"What about the other half?"

"The other half says okay, all kinds of things work if you believe in them. It's good medicine to believe."

"I'm ready, let's go." Carl took the lead up the trail. Finger hooked in the empty bottle of soda pop, he swung it against his leg in time with his steps. He wasn't tired anymore. He'd done all right in the *gallo* race. Maybe he would get to climb Katzimo this summer. Maybe . . .

Carl and Leo returned just before the start of the horse race. In this contest the rooster was buried in the sand on the plains below Ácoma with only his head showing. The participants started on foot from the top of the mesa, tore down the trail, then, still on the run, leaped on their horses and took off. Carl, Leo, and Horace left the rest of the family and ran to the edge of the big rock to look down on the panorama below. They watched the galloping riders jostling one another in the struggle to be first to reach the rooster and pry him loose from his bed of sand.

It was easy to pick out Wilbert from the rest. Although he had exchanged his dancing skirt for trousers, he had not had time to wash the paint from his body nor remove the parrot feathers from his hair. Also, he was riding shaggy Zutu, who was not as handsome as his sleek running mates. But Wilbert had sworn that Zutu would make up for his undistinguished appearance by having more pep than any other six horses at Ácoma.

The group, bunched together at the start, now began to string out. As though to justify his master's faith in him, Zutu, halfway back in the pack of riders thundering toward the buried rooster, suddenly put on a spurt that left a dozen horses trailing him.

"Look, Carl!" Horace yelled excitedly. "Wilbert's going to be first."

But Zutu didn't quite make it in time. The rider ahead of him leaned down, scooped up the flapping rooster, and with a shout of victory was off down the sandy plain. Zutu was hard on his heels, gaining, gaining, until the two horses ran side by side. Wilbert, twisting his body in the saddle, flung out his arms to grab the rooster held on high by the other horseman. Then Wilbert seemed, all at once, to be failing as he

grappled with his opponent for the strange prize. At this distance the blue-green paint on his torso blurred and was obscured in the dust raised by the animal's hoofs.

An involuntary "Oh, no!" escaped from Carl as he lost sight of Wilbert. But the next moment he and Horace were jumping up and down, raising their own cloud of dust. With lightning speed Wilbert and Zutu streaked out from the melee of horses and riders, and Wilbert was holding aloft, in one hand, the precious fowl. Then the whole group was rapidly lost to sight as the pursuit continued far out on the plains and up into the mountains. Carl had been told that the race would continue as long as a shred of rooster remained. It might be one hour or as long as four, depending upon the heart and horsemanship of the contestants.

Late in the afternoon, when the *gallo* racers could be seen coming back across the plains, the girls and women of the pueblo began to leave the group of spectators and hurry to their homes. Carl noticed that his mother was joining her sisters, Plácida and María. When Helen started to go too, he asked, "What are you going to do?"

"We must make ready for the *tse-ai-tee-ah*, the bread-giving. Early this morning the women of Ácoma baked many loaves of bread in different ceremonial shapes. When the riders come down the streets we throw the bread from the second story of our houses. We throw other things too—legs of lamb, *guayave*, peaches, all kinds of gifts. The riders catch what they can and what falls to the ground—well, anybody can take that." Helen laughed at Carl's expression. "You think it is a strange custom, cousin Carl?"

"No, it's just that . . ."

"Just that so many new things have happened to you today, right?" Turning, Helen waved to Carl. "You must come watch the bread-giving so you will remember when you go home to California again."

The sound of hoofs clambering up the horse trail claimed Carl's attention. Laughing and joking with each other and with the crowd, the riders ambled into town. Catching sight of Wilbert, Carl ran to greet him. The parrot feathers had totally disappeared in the heat of the chase. Only the soggy *banda* around the forehead remained. The blue-green paint had almost disappeared. Just a few sweat-streaked daubs showed on Wilbert's forearms. Zutu's shaggy coat was a lathered, tangled mess of burrs and feathers, but both horse and rider looked pleased with themselves.

"Who won?" Carl asked.

"Everybody wins, cousin-brother, and everybody can play. That's what makes it such a good game. It's great if you get a feather or a piece of rooster, but if you don't you can still ride. If you feel mean, you can ride all the meanness out. If you feel happy you can ride until you get happier than you've ever been before. Come on, Carl, let's see if we can catch a loaf of bread. But if we don't, it doesn't matter. There'll be feasting later on with plenty for everyone."

5

Carl Learns
to Take a Punch

Carl had been reluctant to leave Ácoma and return to San Rafael except that he wanted to be with his brother Leo. In recent years Solomon, because of other business interests in San Francisco, had been forced to rely more and more heavily upon Leo to run the trading post. Since Leo had not been to California for some time and Carl had never visited New Mexico until this summer, he had seen little of this older brother.

This first morning at San Rafael, Leo roused him early, calling out like a drill sergeant, "Up and at 'em, Carl. We keep Ácoma hours here too. Comes the dawn and Leo Bibo, the *kahera* of San Rafael, blasts all the eager workers out of bed."

Short and swarthy, packed with energy, Leo had a way of lining people up in a hurry without causing resentment. He had inherited Solomon's gift of tongues, as well as his gift of gab, and no small part of his value to the store lay in his ability to communicate in Spanish and a number of Indian dialects. Breakfast over, the working day began as Leo turned the key in the padlock on the door of the trading post and motioned Carl in ahead of him.

"Go take a look around, Carl, while I set things up for business. The Navaho families camped up there on the hill will be coming over in a little while to do some buying and trading." While Leo talked he moved quickly about the store. "To begin with, we'll put a can of tobacco on this end of the counter so the men can roll themselves a smoke. That's the first rule of etiquette. Then we put a jar of hard candy on the other end so the *maruchas*, the ladies, can help themselves to a piece and give some to the *maruchitos*, the children. Another thing, if you're going to give me a hand while you're here, you'll have to learn never to say to a Navaho, can I show you a hat or a pair of pants? If you offer help when they first come in, nine times out of ten they'll turn around and walk out. When they're ready to trade they'll come to you. That's their way of doing things. The pueblo tribes are just the opposite. They want attention right away." Leo's voice faded as he went into the rear of the store.

Carl picked up the dust cloth Leo had placed on the counter and began to wipe off the scarred wood. He carefully worked around the pound bags of coffee labeled Arbuckle's Ariosa and noticed that, on the floor near the big coffee grinder, there were fifty-pound sacks of the same brand. Piled next to the coffee were huge bags of flour that bore the label, Diamond

M. La Marr Flour Mill, Colorado. Most of the food-stuffs in the store came in giant sizes, but Carl knew that sheepherders and ranchers were often isolated months at a time, especially in winter, and that they had to buy enough to last.

Leo yelled to Carl as he came back carrying a stack of Stetson hats. "Push that stepladder over here and come hold the hats while I put them on the shelf. That's another thing you have to know about Navahos. They're not happy with anything but the finest hats and you better have plenty to choose from. A lot of these folks come from as far as a hundred miles away, bypassing other trading posts to trade with us. That's because pop always gave them a fair deal."

Flipping the hats on the shelf expertly, Leo said, "Reach behind the counter, Carl, and get the feather duster. Then we'll switch places. You get up here and dust off these leather boots and hackamores and I'll break some silver dollars out of the safe. Nobody around here, Indian, Mexican, or Anglo, trusts paper money and you can't blame them for that. Paper doesn't feel right when you're used to the real thing. Also, there's nothing like going into Albuquerque with your pockets bulging with solid silver. It even makes you dance better. Gives you some ballast."

"I wouldn't know about that," Carl said.

"Not yet, but it won't be long."

The door opened and three Navaho men walked in, dressed in the working outfit of Levis, loose shirts, and black Stetsons worn high and round without the center crease in the top. In their arms they carried fur pelts.

"*Ahalani*, hello," Leo said without stopping his work behind the counter. "We haven't seen you since last year."

"*Ahalani*. Where do we put these?" a member of the group asked. "We have all kinds of skins—coyote, fox, skunk, cowhide, goatskin."

"You'd better put them in the back room, there's more space there."

The front door opened again and two Mexican señoras from town entered, carrying baskets on their arms, black wool mantillas draped over heads and shoulders despite the hot summer morning.

"*Buenos días*, Señor Leo, we have fresh eggs right out of the nest. Still warm—feel them. We want to trade them for *harina de maíz*, cornmeal, and pinto beans."

Now the door swung open wide and a whole battalion of Navaho women and children entered. The children were dressed as exact miniatures of their parents. Some of the little girls were so tiny that they seemed barely able to move under the weight of full skirts and heavy velveteen blouses as they toddled to the counter for candy. The *maruchas* headed immediately for the drygoods department to look over the new shipment of calicos from which they made their voluminous skirts. There they would feel, exclaim, and spend hours deciding which colors to buy. One of the boys had a *cabrillo*, a little goat that he pulled along on a frayed rope. The *cabrillo* pulled back to nibble on

the edges of the flour sacks whenever his master's attention wandered, which was often, so that there was a constant tug of war between them.

Across the street Carl saw the blacksmith shop of Antonio Lavo. Señor Lavo, an elderly gentleman, had been a friend of Juana and Solomon since the early days of their marriage. The blacksmith shop was as busy as the trading post. Half a dozen Navahos were waiting for their horses to be shod and to have new rims put on their wagon wheels. Carl watched the aged Antonio in pantomime as he shook his finger at his helper, flung both arms in the air in distress at some problem, then suddenly broke into smiles and ran forward to greet several people who had just pulled up in a truck.

Carl's interest was immediately caught because one of the newcomers was a boy about his own age. He saw his father and mother hurrying across the road, and a whole series of embraces and salutations were exchanged all around. By this time Carl's nose was pressed to the window, staring at the silent scene. Solomon, turning toward the trading post, caught sight of him and motioned him to come out. Carl picked his way past a group of Navaho children seated in the doorway, turning the pages of a Montgomery Ward catalogue. The *maruchitos* were sucking noisily on candy sticks, sharing them unconsciously with the goat, who went from one to another stealing a lick whenever he could.

Walking down the steps of the trading post Carl

could hear his father saying, "But of course Harold can stay here with us until the boxing match is over. We'd be honored to have a future champion of the ring train at San Rafael. The town will never stop talking about it. Yes, Carl will be around for a while before he goes back to Ácoma." As Carl approached the group Solomon called out, "Carl, come here and meet your cousins, Paolo Bibo and his son Harold."

The young cousin was a blue-eyed blond with the kind of ruddy skin that never tans no matter how much exposure it has to the weather. He was short and square and when he talked his words almost ran into each other. Carl would discover that Harold walked fast, talked fast, and thought fast, but that his feelings rarely showed in his face.

While he shook hands Harold said, tumbling his words out, "Hi, Carl, my dad and I are on a buying trip. We're buying cowhides for Healfeld Brothers store in Albuquerque. Your father has a stack of them ready for us. Want to help me load them in the truck?"

"Okay."

"They stink something awful. No matter how much you wash you can't get the smell off once you've handled them. It just has to wear off."

"I don't mind."

"Hold on, hold on," Solomon protested. Turning to Paolo, he said with a smile, "What a boy you've raised there. Look at the way he's got Carl working already. If I asked Carl to do the same thing it would take him half an hour to make up his mind, half an hour to say yes, and another half an hour to lift a finger. But, seriously, boys, we've got a few things to settle first."

At that moment Antonio Lavo called excitedly to Harold's father, "*Venga, por favor*, Señor Paolo. *Tengo aquí un caballo muy enfermo.*"

Seeing Carl's bewilderment at the stream of Spanish, Harold explained, "Señor Lavo wants my dad to help him with a sick horse."

"Is your father a veterinarian?" Carl asked.

"He's better than a vet," Harold said matter-of-factly. "Pueblo people, Mexicans, everybody calls him in from miles around to help with their animals."

In the midst of the confusion Solomon puffed out his cheeks in exasperation. "Ach, this is a typical meeting of the Bibo family. Six things going on at once and nobody making any sense. Juanita, tell Carl what's happening."

As she so often did, Juana stepped quietly into the group and immediately commanded attention. "Carl, your cousin Paolo has a trading post in Mogollon, a mining town high in the mountains. He has to drive on today and take the hides up there for shipment. Harold is going to be in a boxing match here in San Rafael this Saturday night and his father wants him to stay with us and train here for the rest of the week. Paolo will come back on Friday and join us in time for the bout."

Turning to Harold, Carl asked admiringly, "Are you really going to be in a boxing match?"

"Yes."

"Have you ever been in one before?"

"Sure."

"How come?"

"I like it, and besides I need the money. I want to go to New Mexico Military Institute."

"Could you teach me how to box?"

"If a little guy like me can learn, why can't you?" Harold said with authority. "Your arms are long. You should have a good reach."

"Come on," Carl said. "Let's put the skins on the truck, then we'll get your suitcase."

The two cousins worked side by side loading the stack of cowhides into the truck from one of the out-buildings behind the trading post. It was a hot day and with each passing moment Carl found that the aroma of the growing pile of skins became richer and riper. There were so many horseflies clustering, crawling, and regrouping that at times the skins twitched as though they were still alive. Carl was getting dizzy from the stench when he heard Harold call out, "Hey, Carl, stand outside there near the driver's seat. I almost forgot to unload my punching bag and other practice equipment."

With complete disregard, Harold plowed through the seething mass of skins toward the front, sending up a black cloud of flies that headed straight for Carl, the tenderfoot. Carl caught several awkwardly shaped bundles as Harold lowered them but he wasn't able to see what they were, so thick was the swarm around him. At last, when Harold climbed out, the regiment of flies zoomed back and latched onto the unfeeling hides while Carl swatted away the remaining squadron still clinging to his own well-bitten skin.

But the next moment he forgot discomfort as he stared at the equipment before him. "What do you do with all those different things? Can I use them too?"

"Sure," Harold said. "I'll explain when we get them set up. First we've got to find a place to put them."

"There's an old barn down the road that belongs to Señor Lavo the blacksmith. He's real nice. I bet he'd let us use it if we ask him."

"Let's go see him." Harold started across the road.

Carl began to follow, then stopped. He had a mental picture of himself decked out in a gleaming pair of satin trunks. Huge boxing gloves covered his hands and he was about to deliver a tremendous right hook straight to the jaw of his cousin Horace, who was backing away fast. Horace does everything better than me, Carl thought. He can run faster, jump higher, climb quicker, but he's not going to be able to fight better. If Horace gets on me anymore when I go back to Ácoma next week I'll be ready for him.

"Hey, come on," Harold yelled. "What are you standing there for? Let's find Señor Lavo. I've been training every day and I want to get everything ready so I can keep right on tomorrow morning."

"Yeah, sure," Carl said, coming back to reality. "Be right with you."

Señor Lavo answered their request for use of his barn by saying graciously, "Si, señores, mi casa es su *casa.*" Harold explained to Carl that this meant "my house is your house," and that Spanish-speaking people used it as a courteous way to indicate that whatever they possessed, be it little or much, was available at all times to their friends.

As the boys started back to where they had left the equipment, Carl said, "Maybe Leo will help us carry the stuff down to the barn. It's about a half mile down the road."

"We won't have to take Leo away from the store. Quate should be here soon. He'll help us. Look, there he is now." Harold pointed toward the trading post.

A little perplexed, Carl stared at what looked like a boy standing in front of the Bibo store with a bedroll at his feet. "Who's Quate?" He asked Harold.

"Quate is my dad's Indian helper," Harold said, "but when I'm boxing Quate's my trainer and he's always in my corner when I fight. He brings me luck. My dad said Quate was going to hitch a ride and come down here to help me work out the rest of the week. He's really rugged."

When the figure caught sight of Harold and Carl, he picked up his bedroll and started walking toward them. As he drew closer Carl saw that he wasn't a boy at all but an exceptionally short man. He stood no more than four-feet-ten but the crow's feet in the corners of his eyes and the crosshatching of lines over broad cheek bones showed him to be middle-aged.

"Hi, Quate," Harold called. "This is my cousin Carl Bibo from San Francisco. We've got a place to work out already. We were just going to take the equipment down there."

"*Mucho gusto*, pleased to meet you," Quate said. As Carl and Quate shook hands, Carl was aware that Quate was scrutinizing his face as though he were reading a map without being able to locate the particular place that he sought.

"My father is Solomon Bibo. He runs the trading post, but my mother was born on the Ácoma pueblo," Carl volunteered.

"Aha," Quate's bronze face broke into a smile of understanding.

"You can stay with us," Carl said. "We live in the house next door to the trading post. We've got lots of room."

"You are welcome, Señor, to stay with us." It was Juana's voice. She had come out of the house while the introductions were going on.

"Missus, I thank you," Quate said, "but I always bring my bedroll because I don't sleep good unless there's nothing between me and the stars."

"We have a big sleeping porch upstairs in our house," Juana persisted. "There is room for all the men and boys. Between you and the stars there will be only a screen, Señor Quate. The screen keeps out bugs but lets in the breeze. Also, it is always well to be under the same roof with friends."

"The missus words are spoken like a daughter of the land." Quate bowed slightly but still did not say whether he would stay with the Bibos or not. Carl was

91

interested in the contest going on between his mother and Quate and he wondered who would win.

Returning the bow, Juana continued, "And you, Señor Quate, being also an *hijo* of New Mexico, have wisely decided to honor us with your company. And now, you will bring your bedroll upstairs, please."

Carl had to hold back a smile at the polite order. But Quate, even if defeated, was not to be outdone in courtesy. "Missus," he said, "it is Quate who is honored by this pleasant invitation."

Juana walked back up the steps in her unhurried way, but before she opened the door she added, "And you will further honor us, of course, by taking meals with us. I will lay another place at the table right now." The door closed, giving her the final word and cutting off any further discussion of this new subject. Quate seemed satisfied with the arrangements and Carl had the impression that his mother and Quate had thoroughly enjoyed the exchange and both had known the outcome in advance.

After supper that evening Quate ordered Harold to bed at eight o'clock and Carl was surprised to see that Harold took this as a matter of course, bid everybody good night, and started up to the sleeping porch without protest.

"Harold, you be outside tomorrow morning about five for a little road work. I'll be waiting for you," Quate called. Then turning to Carl, he said, "You feeling strong, you wanna go along?"

"Sure."

"Okay, then you better get to bed early too. Me, I wanna walk down the road and take a look at the recreation hall where the fight's gonna be held."

"I'll go with you," Solomon said. "When Juanita makes enchiladas I always need a walk after dinner."

After the two men left, the house was quiet. Leo had driven into Albuquerque to see one of his girl friends and Juana was in the kitchen supervising the cleaning up. Carl knew he ought to get to bed too if he wanted to keep up tomorrow with the rigorous training schedule that Quate had indicated at dinner. He was determined to last out the whole day, not only because he really wanted to know how to box but also because of the good-natured teasing he had taken from Leo at dinner. When Carl had expressed his desire to work out with Harold and Quate the rest of the week Leo had laughed and said, "So, I lose my helper in the store already. But you don't know what you're getting into, little brother. Anytime you feel so tired you can't skip rope another minute, you can always use me as an excuse. Just tell Quate that I need you in the store."

Everybody laughed but Carl, as he muttered, "I might get tired but I won't give up."

From the kitchen Juana called, "Carl, get your dirty clothes together that you brought from Ácoma. Consuelo washes tomorrow. I think you left your suitcase downstairs in Leo's room."

Carl whipped into Leo's room to do the chore with a haste that was unlike him. He had suddenly remembered that his diary was in the suitcase along with his clothes and he didn't want his mother to unpack his things and find it. He had included in his account of the riding lessons at the pueblo his feelings about Horace. But fast as he was, he wasn't fast enough. He had half the contents of the suitcase on the floor and the other half on the bed along with the diary when his mother entered the room with a straw clothes basket in her arms.

"Let's put them in here," she said, plucking clothes from the bed.

"Now wait a minute, mom. Leave the clothes basket here and I'll fill it up and bring it into the kitchen. Some of it's clean. I haven't sorted it out yet."

"Are you worried about this?" Juana held up the diary. "I won't read it, but tell me, *hijo mio*, have you had time to write anything in it yet?"

"Once at Ácoma I got up before dawn and wrote about Wilbert teaching me to ride a horse. I really like him, mom. He's one of the greatest guys I ever met."

"And Horace?" Juana asked quietly.

"Horace—well, he's different."

"But do you like him?"

"Sometimes I do, but I don't think he likes me much. Sometimes he'll act okay, then the next minute he turns around and tries to make me look dumb or he says something mean."

"You got along on San Juan's Day."

"Yeah, because I really worked at it. I don't think he likes Anglos very much, even half an Anglo like me. Nobody else at Ácoma acts that way, only him."

94

"Do you want to go back to Ácoma again this summer?" Juana asked.

"Of course. It's neat there. I'm going back next week in time for the rainmakers' dance. Wilbert says it's something I ought to see. Besides I'm—" But Carl didn't finish the sentence because the end of it was, I'm going to be ready to beat Horace to a pulp if he starts in on me again.

"Tomorrow—" Juana cradled the basket in her arms as she walked toward the door—"Leo is driving to Ácoma in the truck to invite my sisters to visit us here for the weekend. Whenever I am in San Rafael, Plácida and María come to spend some time. It is very interesting to them because it is as far as they have ever been in their whole lives."

"You mean they've never even been to Albuquerque?"

Juana shook her head, "No, never. This will be a very special visit. Friday we will celebrate the Sabbath eve with a family dinner. Harold's father Paolo will be back then too. Saturday night we will all go to the boxing match."

"That sounds great, mom," Carl said.

Juana stepped through the doorway. "Wilbert and Helen will come too." Then she looked back at Carl. "—and Horace. Good night, Carlitos."

Next morning, when Carl went outside to join Quate and Harold, he noticed a peculiar smell in the air that was totally unlike anything he had ever encountered before. He saw Quate pouring a thick, gray-green substance into the palms of Harold's hands.

"Rub it in good," Quate said. "Does it still hurt?"

"It just sort of tingles anymore." Harold kneaded the gooey stuff into his knuckles.

"Good, it's doing the job. When the skin is a hundred percent tough you won't feel it at all."

"What's the matter? Did you cut yourself?" Carl asked.

"This is part of Quate's treatment to toughen up my hands for the fight."

Wrinkling up his nose, Carl sniffed the bottle. "Sure smells awful. What is it?"

"I don't know. Quate won't tell anybody."

"Smells like it has varnish in it." Carl looked inquiringly at Quate.

"Maybe," Quate said with an innocent smile.

Carl sniffed again. "And gunpowder."

"Maybe." Quate shrugged his shoulders.

"Even if you guessed right he wouldn't tell you," Harold said. "It's a secret formula. I think he brews it out of rattlesnake milk, sandía chiles, and coyote spit."

Quate laughed uproariously. "That's the closest you ever came. Okay, *chicos*, boys, we gonna do a little running now, then breakfast, then we really go to work."

Quate set a moderate pace and the boys followed after. Carl had no trouble keeping up. Although he wasn't fast, his long legs were supple and strong from tennis and hiking, so the early morning workout was a pleasure not a punishment. As they jogged along Quate hummed a strange song that was punctuated by sounds that were so much like those of a hoot owl that, at first, Carl looked around him, wondering how come a night bird would be out in broad daylight.

Quate, obviously enjoying Carl's bewilderment, said, "You like my song, huh? That's an Apache chant to the mountain spirits. It'll keep everybody healthy and bring good luck in the fight."

After breakfast the three of them walked down to the old barn that Señor Lavo was allowing them to use. The practice equipment was set up, and last night Carl had learned that Harold, Paolo, and Quate had made all of it. There were two kinds of punching bags. The fast bag, used for timing, was made out of an old-fashioned, round rubber football over which a canvas cover had been stitched. This was hung from a beam. The heavy bag, which was long and shaped like the kind used for tackle practice, had been dreamed up from feed sacks, then stuffed with sawdust. Harold said the reason it had battle scars all over was because when it split and started to leak, Quate darned it with heavy thread. Sometimes the heavy bag was fastened to the floor but because of the temporary setup this one wasn't. The first time Carl tried it, Quate held on to the other side to keep it from moving. The moment Carl began to swing Quate bellowed like an old bull.

"You a southpaw or something? No? Then lead with your left, lead with your left." Each time Quate let fly with his orders the cows at the other end of the barn set up a mournful mooing in protest.

Carl thought Harold looked great in his boxing trunks and he envied him a pair of biceps as big around as a fellow twice his age. But Quate looked Harold up and down, his expression unimpressed, before he said, "You better get on the heavy bag. Your muscles look like a *ristra*."

Carl knew that a *ristra* was one of those long strings of dried chiles that hang outside every adobe house in New Mexico. He couldn't help smile but he didn't dare laugh. He had the feeling that Quate could say anything to Harold and it would be okay, but if anyone else opened his mouth he might be flattened in a minute.

"And another thing," Quate went on, "I thought up a good ring name for you. Battling Bibo, how's that? But you better live up to it because I hear that this kid you're going to fight Saturday night, this *chico* from the town of Datil, is ten pounds heavier than you and a couple inches taller. He's supposed to be plenty tough."

After a while Carl wanted to try the fast bag. It looked like more fun and less work, but Quate said, "Uh-uh, not yet. The heavy bag is for beginners."

Carl tried to argue with him. "This equipment won't be here long enough for me to be anything but a beginner. I've got to learn in a hurry."

Quate gave Carl one of his cool looks, then he said, "Whatsamatter, you got some fellow you want to beat up?"

Carl, startled by the way Quate had figured out his motives for learning to fight, punched the bag harder and harder until Quate yelled, "No more punching with bare knuckles. You'll split 'em wide open. Wait 'til Harold starts with the jump rope and he'll lend you his bag gloves."

Carl finally got a small compliment out of Quate. He caught on to the rope skipping with no problem. Again, tennis helped. Quate watched him for a minute then he said, "Not bad for the first time. Maybe after three, four months you could even be fast on your feet." To Harold he said, "Suck in your gut. You been eating too many soda pops and ice creams." Then he added, "The left hook is good." But in case Harold might get a swelled head, his last words were, before declaring the session over, "Your timing's lousy."

Leo had slipped in quietly before the end of the workout, but now that he saw it was over, he called out, "Mom is helping dad in the store and they told me to come down here and take you guys out for lunch. We'll go to the cafe down the road. We'll have to. It's the only one in town."

Leo had driven over in the truck and as they piled in he said, "Are the Bibos ever getting famous! I was at Ácoma today and they even know about the fight over there. Everybody in San Rafael is laying bets.

You'd think that Harold was going to be the star of the main bout instead of the preliminary."

Carl couldn't help asking, "Does Horace know?"

"The whole pueblo knows."

As they sat down at the counter in the cafe Harold said in his rapid way, "I'm starving. I want four tacos, two glasses of milk, custard, and a bowl of *pozole*."

"What's *pozole*?" Carl asked.

"It's green corn cooked with chile," Harold explained. "It only costs a nickel and you get a lot of it."

"Whatever it is, bring it on," Carl said. "I could eat an ox. I'm starving too."

Carl and Harold stuffed themselves until their plates were as bare as the clean ones stacked up behind the counter. The *pozole* was so hot that Carl's eyes watered and his nose ran, but he just kept sniffling and stowing it away. When he finished, his throat felt like he'd swallowed the flaming sword at the circus. While he gulped a whole glass of water he watched a Mexican boy, with a *banda* tied around his head, frying tortillas and stuffing them with a strange-looking kind of meat.

Carl said to Quate, "Is that what we ate? What is that gunk he's putting in the tortillas?"

"Horse meat, probably. Best thing you can eat when you're in training, that and venison. There's no fat on it," Quate said matter-of-factly.

Slapping some money down on the counter, Leo

eased himself off the stool. "I've got to go. I told pop I wouldn't be long. You want to ride back with me, Quate? Looks like these kids are going to go on eating forever."

"Okay," Quate said. "Harold, you be back at the barn at two o'clock."

While the two boys waited for their custard, Carl said, "Quate sure knows everything about boxing. He told me when all the champions were born, how many fights they had, who they fought, the whole works back for a hundred years. He must spend all his time reading up on it when he isn't working."

"He can't read," Harold said.

"Then where does he get the information? Did he used to box?"

"Never, as far as my dad and I can find out. He's smart and he has a memory like an encyclopedia. He listens to ring talk and files the information away. Ask him anything. You'll always get an answer and if you check on him you'll find out he's right."

"The fight's only three days away," Carl said. "How do you feel about it?" Harold's face got that blank, no-soap look. "It's like any other fight."

Carl wanted to ask if Harold had ever fought anyone that much taller and heavier than himself but he figured he'd better let it drop. From what he'd seen so far, Harold wasn't likely to reveal what was going on in his head nor to appreciate anybody prying into it. Instead, Carl asked, "Are you going to be a professional boxer?"

"No, I want to go to college after I get through New Mexico Military Institute. Come on, let's go, Quate gets sore if he's kept waiting."

The boys were about to open the door when a tall, hollow-faced man wearing a wide-brimmed black hat and a long black coat with tails on it like an undertaker, grabbed hold of Harold's arm.

"You're Bibo, aren't you?" he asked.

"That's right."

"I came down here from Mogollon for the main bout but I see on the posters around town that you're going to fight in the curtain raiser. I won some money off a fellow at the Little Fannie mine the other day so I'm going to bet on you. Put up a good fight and I'll really toss in the silver. I'm loaded."

"Thanks," Harold murmured, then broke away and walked through the door.

When they were out of earshot Carl said, "Who was that?"

"He hangs around Mogollon all the time where my dad has his store. He's a professional gambler. You can always tell by the soft hands. All they do is deal cards."

"He's dressed up like he's going to be in a vaudeville show."

"He always looks like that. It's part of the act."

"Does he really have a lot of money?"

Harold pointed to his head. "Up here, yes." Then he pointed to his pockets. "Down here, no. He's an old windbag."

But Carl was impressed. As they walked back to the

barn he tried to imagine what it would be like to have somebody know that you were a fighter and recognize you in a public place. It was the neatest thing he could think of and it was going to make a great story to tell to the folks at Ácoma, especially Horace.

For the next few days Carl lived, ate, and slept boxing. Quate got tougher and tougher with each session, yelling his orders until Carl wondered how he could keep from losing his voice. During the early morning road work he'd shout, "Run light and fast like an Apache, not heavy and slow like Anglos. I'll tell you when to switch to a walk and when I do, make it heel and toe. No slopping along or you might as well stay home and shoot marbles."

During the afternoon Quate acted as sparring partner for Harold. Shorter than his twelve-year-old pupil, Quate threw punches while Harold practiced side-stepping and ducking.

"Too bad you don't know more about boxing," Quate said to Carl. "You're about as tall as the fellow Harold's going to box Saturday night. If Harold's father, Señor Paolo, was here he'd stand in so Harold could get a real workout with someone the right height."

Carl discovered that it was Harold's father who had first instructed his son in the art of boxing, when Harold was barely old enough to put on a pair of gloves. Quate often started his instructions to Harold with, "Señor Paolo says you should—" and Harold always listened carefully, seldom talked back, and, to

Carl's inexperienced eyes, put the orders into effect promptly and efficiently.

On the Friday afternoon before the fight the training session was short and Quate announced solemnly that there would be no workout on Saturday morning. As they packed up the practice equipment, Quate explained why.

"It's no good to be over-trained. Harold can go on a little hike tomorrow if he wants, maybe three, four miles, enough to loosen up the legs, but otherwise he should stay off the punching bag and think about something else, something nice like all that money he might get if he fights good enough. Of course it won't pay off like the Dempsey-Gibbons fight in Shelby, Montana, a couple years back, but those silver cartwheels add up if the crowd throws enough of them."

Just before they took down the heavy bag, Carl took a final swat at it, hating to see it packed away.

"Hey, Carl," Quate said, flipping the bag on his back as though it were filled with feathers, "I got something special for you but I got to check it out with Señor Paolo when he comes in tonight. You been a pretty good sport and maybe you even learned a little besides. You deserve a nice reward." Quate chuckled to himself as he slid the bag into a crate.

Carl's smile was doubtful. He wasn't sure what Quate's idea of something special might be.

"Come on, boys," Quate called. "Leo's here with the truck." As Carl hopped in beside Quate, the little man winked at him and said, "You'll see, *chico*. You gonna like my surprise."

6

The Runaway

As Leo turned the truck onto the main street of San Rafael, he was forced to slow down because of the cloud of dust raised by the wagon plodding ahead of them. Through the haze Carl could see that the wagon was loaded to the brim with muskmelons, sacks of red chiles, onions, and corn. A boy on horseback rode beside it, his long black hair swinging back over his shoulders with the jounce of the high-stepping pony, who seemed impatient with the slow pace. The pony's coat was rough and shaggy, and suddenly Carl exclaimed, "That's Zutu, with Wilbert riding him! It must be the folks from Ácoma in the wagon ahead of us."

In a few seconds the horses pulled over to the side of the road and obeying a "whoa, there" from the driver, stopped near a hitching post as though from long habit. A slim figure jackknifed over the back of the wagon and Carl leaned out the truck, calling, "Hey, Horace, it's me, Carl."

Horace raised his hand in brief salute, then went about the business of hitching up the horses. People began to spill out of the wagon at the same time that the door to Solomon Bibo's trading post opened and Carl heard his mother exclaim, "Sol, come along. Plácida and María are here with the children, and I think that is Paolo pulling up now behind Leo's truck. Everybody's arrived at once."

In the midst of the milling about, Carl found himself alongside Horace, helping to unload the wagon.

"Horace—" Carl raised his voice above the din—"I want you to meet my cousin, Harold Bibo. He's going to fight here in San Rafael tomorrow night. I've been working out with him every day. He and Quate, his trainer, have been teaching me how to box too. It's a lot of fun. You ought to try it sometime and you ought to see the equipment we used. Two kinds of punching bags and a lot of other stuff. Too bad it's packed away now." Carl was boasting and he knew it, but Horace was beginning to have this effect on him. Because Horace ignored him so pointedly most of the time, Carl tried to make himself felt in ways that were unlike him.

"Hello, Harold. Haven't seen you for quite a while," Horace said. "Hope you win the fight tomorrow night." Horace swung a sack of corn over his shoulder, then, turning to Carl, he added, "You don't need to introduce me to Harold, I knew him a long time before you ever did. But you wouldn't think about that, would you? Like you don't think about most things."

Carl felt it was a good thing he had started to lift

a heavy basket of muskmelons because if his hands had been free he might have taken a poke at Horace right then and there in front of everybody. It wasn't only Horace's words that annoyed him but his tone of voice and the implication, always present, that he, Carl, was a dummy. He knew he was angry far beyond the cause and that he had provoked part of it. That made him even madder, at himself. His fingers fumbled with the basket and, as he made a desperate clutch, he felt the weight steadied by another pair of hands and heard Wilbert say quickly, "Hang on, cousin-brother. These melons don't bounce when they hit the ground. They split wide open in a thousand pieces. We missed you at Ácoma but I hear you'll be going back with us on Sunday. Next week we prepare for the rainmakers' dance. We have many things to do before you return to San Francisco and not much time to do them in. The summer flies fast on the wings of an eagle, the winter creeps slow on the paws of a porcupine."

As they set the basket down beside the kitchen door, Carl said, "Thanks for the help, Wilbert. I've learned how to box since I've been here at San Rafael. I'm not real good at it yet but I know how to train."

"I want to hear about that," Wilbert said seriously, wiping his hands off on his blue cotton overalls.

Suddenly the back door opened and Juana looked out. "Carl, Wilbert, call the others to come along now and get cleaned up before sundown. We have to be ready for the Sabbath eve."

The Solomon Bibo family did not make a religious observance every Friday night, although special holy days were kept throughout the year—Yom Kippur, the Day of Atonement, and Passover, the Festival of Unleavened Bread. But since the family had become so widely scattered, Solomon and Juana felt that when they gathered a group of members together in their home, and this coincided with the coming of the Sabbath, it was a special occasion to be marked by thanksgiving.

The ceremony of the Saturday Sabbath, the Jewish day of rest, is in remembrance of the creation of the world by God. Just before sundown the family gathered in the dining room, awaiting Juana's entrance. By the time the door opened the lively group was completely silent. Juana walked in, dressed, as was her custom, in ceremonial buckskins of snowy white and wearing her most elaborate turquoise and silver jewelry. She always honored her husband's faith by donning the outfit that also symbolized the highest respect that one could accord her native Indian religion.

The long dining table was laid with a fresh white cloth. At one end an empty wine cup and an unlit candelabra had been placed beside a small hand-woven square, the size of a napkin, used to cover the two loaves of freshly baked *hallah*, the twisted bread that is part of the Sabbath meal. Tradition assigns the ceremony of the candles to the mother of the family because her mission is to kindle the light of the

Torah, the sacred laws and teachings, in the hearts of her children. As she leaned over to light the candles, Juana said, "Thou art our light, O Lord, and our Salvation. In Thy Name we kindle these Sabbath lights. May they bring into our household the beauty of truth and the radiance of love's understanding. On this Sabbath eve, and at all times, let there be light."

Juana relinquished her place at the head of the table to Solomon, who signaled that all should be seated. Solomon began to recite the Kiddush, the prayer of sanctification that ushers in the Sabbath and major holidays. At its conclusion he filled the wine cup and lifted it saying, "Praised be Thou, Lord our God, King of the Universe, who hast created the fruit of the vine."

Sipping the wine, he passed the glass around the table, each, in turn, drinking from it. Then Solomon pronounced the final benediction. "May the God of our fathers bless you. May He who has guided us unto this day lead you to be an honor to our family and all mankind." Heads were bowed as Solomon paused for a moment before adding, "And in conclusion let us heed the words of the great sage Hillel who phrases the golden rule in a different way: Do not do unto your friend what is hateful unto you. Amen."

There was a brief silence, then Solomon said, "Now we eat, and I can hear the children mumbling their own little prayer which goes, thank the Lord for that."

The dinner was a mixture of many traditions. Down the center of the table matzohs, unleavened bread, alternated with *guayave*, the unleavened cere- monial bread of the Ácomas. Chicken and *farfel*, a tiny noodle of German origin, was served with deer jerky brought from the pueblo. It was a happy crowd and although the languages spoken were as varied as the food, the laughter was universal.

"What a ruckus," the hospitable Solomon said, beaming at everyone. "Never have I seen such gab- bling and gobbling except at a turkey ranch. Eat hearty. The food is good and so is the company."

Though they were seated across from each other, Carl and Horace had not exchanged a single word throughout the meal, but the general gaiety covered the lack of communication. Carl had glanced at his cousin at the conclusion of the prayers when Solomon said, Do not do unto your friend what is hateful unto you. He hoped the advice was registering, but Hor- ace's bowed head gave no indication of what was going on inside.

Suddenly Solomon rapped on the table. "Quiet please. Señor Quate, the rough and rugged gentleman who trains champions, has an announcement to make."

Standing up, Quate bowed to his hosts, Solomon and Juana. "First, I want to thank the mister and the missus of this house for having me to sit down at their feast day, which I like very much. Next, I want to make an invitation to their son Carl and this is what it

110

is. Always when Harold fights, Señor Paolo and me are together in his corner. A little while ago I checked with Señor Paolo and we figured that, instead, Carl might like to help me out tomorrow night. It would give him something special to tell those San Francisco *chicos* when he goes home."

"Me?" Carl said, the corners of his mouth quivering into a smile.

"Right," Quate said. "You wanna help?"

"Sure I do, but I don't know anything about it."

"You will," Quate said with the complete assurance that was characteristic of him when the subject was boxing. "I'll tell you all you have to know before the fight tomorrow."

As Quate sat down, Carl stole a look across the table at Horace. His face was unreadable as he crumbled a piece of *guayave* bread into a little pile on the tablecloth, swept it into his plate, and immediately began to crumble another. He didn't look up once during dessert, nor did he eat any more, refusing melon and pie.

He's jealous, Carl thought, and for a second he was glad. But the next minute he thought, I'd be jealous too. Just then he caught his mother's eye. Juana looked across the table at Horace then back at Carl, repeating the action several times. It was clear to Carl that the message she was sending read: This is your home and these are your guests. You are a host. Behave like one.

Carl tried to think of something to say to Horace

to draw him out of his silence. Making conversation, his sisters called it. I guess I haven't had enough practice at it, he thought. The only thing I can think of right now is the fight tomorrow night and that's not a good subject. Fortunately the problem was taken out of his hands because, at the other end of the table, Leo had started describing to Paolo and Harold his difficulties in obtaining an overhead valve assembly for an engine he had rebuilt.

The automobile was still enough of a novelty so that everybody fell silent as Leo explained, "I finally sent back to Laurel, Maryland, for it, installed it in my Model T, and now I make more than seventy-five miles an hour, even on dirt roads. Tell you what, how would you kids like to have a ride in it after dinner?"

"Can I go too?" cousin Helen asked.

"Sure, why not?"

"Class dismissed," Solomon said. "The old folks will sit here and let the meal digest quietly. Leo, be careful. Don't forget it's dark now and even in full daylight those roads outside of town are mean."

"Don't worry, pop, I won't let her go full speed."

"And don't keep Harold out too long," Paolo added. "He has to have a good night's sleep."

Leo's car was parked outside the trading post. "You can all get in if you squeeze hard enough," Leo called. "Carl and Helen better come up front with me."

As Carl started toward the car he noticed Horace standing in the shadows, making no move to get in. Harold had already climbed into the back seat, while

Wilbert stood there holding the door ajar, waiting for Horace.

"I'll stay here," Horace said in a low voice.

"Get in," Wilbert said firmly. "Don't keep Leo waiting."

But Horace still hung back. It was dark and, though Carl could not make out the expressions on the faces of the two young men, he could feel the clash of wills.

"Hey, what's holding us up? Are we ready?" Leo called.

Neither Horace nor Wilbert had moved an inch. Then Carl heard Wilbert say something in Ácoma that rang out like a command, and with that Horace reluctantly got in the car.

Wilbert's the only one who can handle him, Carl thought. What makes Horace act like that anyway? Then he remembered his mother saying, why don't you ask him some time, and he decided he might do that if the right moment ever arose.

As they pulled away from the store, the rollicking strains of a popular Mexican folk song called "*El Viejo*," "The Old Man," could be heard in the distance and a wagon drawn by horses rounded the corner ahead of them.

Helen cried out, "Please stop. Let's hear the music."

There were three musicians seated on chairs in the wagon, the scene illuminated by lanterns placed on the floor. One man played a guitar, another an accordion, the last a cornet. They were dressed in the elaborate Mexican riding outfits used on fiesta days—sombreros, hats with huge brims turned up all around, tight black jackets, and trousers decorated with braid and embroidery. The rhythm of the tune was infectious. Leo beat time with his palms on the steering wheel, while the rest of them tapped with their feet or snapped their fingers. All except Horace.

Glancing back at him, Carl saw that he sat motionless, hands clasped between his knees, eyes riveted to the floor. It was the classic position of resentful obedience assumed by every boy when a hated order had to be complied with. Carl knew exactly how Horace was feeling and, for a moment, he sympathized with him. Then he lost patience, remembering that when he was at Ácoma he hadn't expected to be in the *gallo* race either, but he had agreed because it was expected. As a visitor, it was the only thing he could do.

The wagon was stopping next to them and a crowd started to gather round. The man with the guitar stood up and began to bellow the words of the song in a voice loud enough to draw people out of their homes and onto the streets.

> They all say I'm a useless old fellow
> But I know not by what they can score.
> For I find myself merry and mellow
> And quite fit for three marriages more.

The verses went on and on. People joined in the singing and a few young couples began to dance in the street. At the conclusion of the number the crowd applauded loud and long, but the musicians shook their heads, indicating with their thumbs that they had to move on.

"*Hola*, Petronillo," Leo called, "*Cuando tendremos el baile?*"

"*Mañana por la noche á la Valencia en Grants,*" the guitar player called back.

"I asked him when the dance was going to be," Leo explained. "He said tomorrow night at the Valencia hall in the nearby town of Grants. Petronillo Gabuldon, the leader, is my friend. He brings his players from Albuquerque and this is the way they advertise. They'll play on the streets of all the villages around here."

"I love the music. It's so happy," Helen said. "I wish we could hear some more."

Starting up the car again, Leo said, "Why don't we all go tomorrow night? Whole families come and spend the evening. The dancing goes on and on. Harold can come too if we go after the boxing match. We can make a night of it."

Carl could imagine how this suggestion was going down with Horace but this time he didn't blame him. A bunch of people dancing around just for the sake of dancing seemed pretty silly. He had watched his sister Celia and her friends when she had parties at home in San Francisco.

"I can't go," Harold said quickly. "My dad and Quate and I have to head for Albuquerque real early Sunday morning."

Glad that Harold had taken the lead, Carl added, "Then I don't want to go."

"Neither do I," Horace said flatly.

"That leaves you and me, Wilbert," Leo said cheerfully. "How about it? You can dance longer and better than any twenty guys I've ever seen."

"I'll go and we'll take Helen too if Aunt Plácida will let her come along."

"Okay, that's settled. Hold on to your hats. I'm going to pick up a little speed now."

Throughout the rest of the drive Horace was completely silent. When they returned to the house in San Rafael he was the first one out of the car. So swiftly and quietly did he move that Carl lost sight of him almost at once. When they walked into the house all the adults except Juana were playing cards in the parlor. Solomon and Quate were carrying on a running fire of humorous asides that diverted the rest of the players, enabling the voluble pair to pile up a big score. Juana greeted the young people and motioned them into the dining room where she had set out a pitcher of pinole, a cornmeal drink, and dishes of ice cream.

"Sit down, everybody. I know you young ones are hungry again. Leo, wind up the victrola, maybe your cousins would like to hear some of those new records from San Francisco."

116

From the parlor Paolo called out, "Harold, time for bed. No ice cream, no pinole tonight. Tomorrow's the big day."

Harold said good night and was gone in a minute, a chorus of "good luck" following him up the stairway.

Juana had been looking around the table counting noses when she said, "Where's Horace? Carl, go look for him and tell him his ice cream is melting."

Not sure of the reception he would get, Carl went in search of Horace. But nobody was upstairs on the screened-in porch that the boys were sharing for sleeping quarters except Harold, who was just turning in and said he hadn't seen Horace. Carl glanced in the other bedrooms, then went down the backstaircase and out the kitchen door. The stars shone with the luminous intensity of a true New Mexico summer night where the combination of mountains and desert produce an extra clarity in the air.

Behind the trading post, up on the hill, a group of Navahos were camped on the site that Solomon always kept especially for them and their families. They liked privacy and appreciated knowing that when they came long distances to trade, this spot was set aside. Carl could see several of the men seated around the campfire playing their own card game of *conquian*. In the shadows someone singing a chant-song to the Yei, the gods of the Navaho, in a mournful falsetto voice. High-pitched sounds were believed to increase the healing power of a prayer

sung for one who was sick. The shrill plaintive notes and the rapidly chilling air sent a shiver down Carl's back.

Below the campsite, Solomon had fenced in a corral for their horses. Carl walked over to it, knowing that the family's wagon from Ácoma was there too, thinking that perhaps Horace had climbed in and fallen asleep. Spotting the wagon, he looked inside but it was empty except for a few corn husks that had spilled from overladen sacks. He stood there feeling that something was missing but not knowing what it was. There were the horses that had pulled the wagon, standing docilely, heads bowed in the moonlight. There was—no, that was it.

"He must have taken Zutu," Carl said aloud.

Carl heard someone coming through the yard. "Cousin-brother—" It was Wilbert's voice. "You were away so long that Aunt Juana sent me in search of you."

"Zutu's gone and I can't find Horace anywhere. Maybe he rode back to Ácoma."

"When we go back in the house," Wilbert said slowly, "let me say that I talked with Horace and that he had forgotten something he had to do at the pueblo. I will also say, to cover up for him, that I told him to go ahead and take Zutu. Aunt Juana may not believe it, because she sees very clearly, but she will pretend to believe so that the other *nawaititra*, the grown-ups, won't be worried and ask too many questions."

"All right," Carl said, "but why did he do it? What's eating him, Wilbert?"

"I don't know."

"You mean he hasn't even told you?"

"Ever since he went to school in Santa Fe he's been different. I don't know what happened there but it must have been something bad. He didn't want to go back. By then we had our own school in Ácomita so he didn't have to. Maybe if I was very wise, like a medicine man, I could look into the *m'caiyoyo*, the rock crystal, and see what it is that hurts him."

"But you'd think he'd want to see the fight tomorrow night."

"He has his own fight," Wilbert said slowly, "going on inside him all the time. But maybe he'll come back."

Suddenly the jingle-jangle of a popular song, "Crazy Rhythm," blared into the night. Someone had opened the door of the house and the tinny strains of the jazz number, played on the victrola, mingled strangely with the weird shrill sounds still coming from the Navaho camp on the hillside.

"Let's go in." Wilbert said. "They're starting to look for us."

When they entered the house Wilbert quickly invented some chores that Horace had forgotten to do at Ácoma. Aunt Plácida looked surprised but made no comment.

Juana asked, "Do you think he'll come back?"

"He didn't know for sure," Wilbert answered,

"He said it depends on how long it takes to finish his work."

"I see," Juana said quietly, and let it go at that.

"I think I'll turn in now," Carl said when he finished his ice cream. "I better get lots of sleep so I can remember what I'm supposed to do tomorrow."

"Spoken like a real champ," Quate called in from the parlor where the card game was still going on. "But sleep tight. Quate always has plenty of ways to make sure a fight goes good, you'll see."

Carl didn't quite understand this statement but he had absolute faith in Quate so he asked for no explanations.

The preliminary bout known as the "curtain raiser" was scheduled for 8:30 P.M. Saturday. About five o'clock Saturday afternoon the family sat down to an early supper. Out of the corner of his eye Carl watched in amazement as Harold stowed away a quart of milk and a half dozen thick slices of roast lamb. Even as a noncombatant Carl was excited enough to find small quantities of food hard to get down.

"Okay, Carl," Quate said at the conclusion of the meal, "now remember what I tell you. Here are the rules. In these curtain raisers we got three rounds, two minutes each. During the round the seconds can't talk to their boxers, make signals with the hands, or give advice on what to do. Also we got to keep our seats during the round. If Harold gives a good wallop or takes one, don't stand up, don't shout, don't make any sound. Otherwise leave everything up to me. If I want you to hand me water, or towels, or anything else I'll say so. Got that?"

"I think so," Carl said, going over it in his mind, then repeating the instructions aloud while Quate nodded his head.

"I haven't seen a fight in ten years, "Solomon said. "At ringside, that is. I've seen plenty of them at roadside in San Rafael with no referee, no rules, and no rounds. When I was younger I took part in a few myself. *Mazel tov*, Harold. That means good luck in Hebrew."

"I think we'll go over now," Paolo said, folding up his napkin. "I want to stake out some ringside seats for the family."

At seven-thirty they began to walk down the road to the recreation hall. They were an odd-looking quartette. Carl did a double-take when he saw Quate's outfit. He had tied the traditional red *banda* around his short black hair, although Carl had never seen him wear it before. His tight red satin shirt studded with pearl buttons was the flashy kind worn by cowboys performing at a rodeo. Over Quate's arm hung a pail filled with salves, lotions, sticking plasters, and other mysterious jars and bottles.

Paolo carried towels and boxing gloves. Carl was allotted the stools. Harold was the only one who wasn't toting something, but he was muffled to the ears in an ancient, well-worn bathrobe that was so many sizes too large for him that he almost stumbled on it when

122

he walked. Carl wondered where he had dug it up. He knew that Harold had a better one than that. He had seen him wearing it around the house.

The last streaks of a fiery sunset were fading from the sky as they entered the rear door of the recreation hall. The first thing Carl noticed when his eyes became accustomed to the gloomy interior was a tall, broad-shouldered youth, standing with his back to them, in earnest conversation with a cigar-chewing older man who seemed to be his handler.

Suddenly the lights came on above the improvised ring and the young man turned around. The glare highlighted well-developed chest muscles, long arms, and sleek black trunks. His step was bouncy as he made his way toward ringside and there was an air of professional assurance about him when he paused to shadowbox, then did a few knee bends to loosen up.

"The kid's really built," Quate murmured. "Harold's gonna have a scrap on his hands."

"You mean that's the fellow he's going to fight?" Carl asked.

"That's him."

Carl glanced at Harold to see his reaction but Harold seemed preoccupied with unwinding the lengthy bathrobe.

"Come on, Carl," Quate said. "Help me get ready."

The rickety old building was starting to fill up. Sporting events like this were rare in San Rafael, so the crowd included ranchers and cowboys who had come from afar. Many local families had brought baskets of sandwiches or tacos, making a picnic as well as an evening's entertainment. So small was the population of the town that some people even recognized Carl, the newcomer, and waved to him. Grinning with pleasure, Carl waved back, enjoying the reflected glory rubbing off on him from being in Harold's corner. Paolo pointed out a group of miners come down from Mogollon where he had his trading post. They were rough but amiable fellows, eager to let off steam after weeks of back-breaking labor in the dark, dank shafts of the silver mines, and they made it clear that Harold was their favorite. Ninety percent of the chatter was in Spanish mixed with various Indian dialects.

As Carl scanned the faces in the hall, he realized that he was looking for Horace as well as looking at the colorful spectators. He was still hoping that Horace would show up in time for the fight but he knew that his motives were mixed. On the positive side was the wish that Horace too might enjoy an exciting experience. On the negative side was the desire to show off, wanting Horace to see how smoothly he, Carl, was following Quate's instructions and how important the job was that he was doing. Carl realized that he was thinking about Horace much more than he wanted to and he was glad to have his train of thought broken when he heard Quate say, "Carl, gimme the sponge." Then, "Wait a minute. Hold it."

Carl saw a familiar figure leaning over to whisper

124

something in Quate's ear. It was the professional gambler from Mogollon.

Quate murmured, "All right. Sure, I'll tell him." Then he waved the man away. When he was gone Quate said to Carl, "The old guy says to tell Harold that the *guapo*, the handsome boy, has never had a bout before, but I wouldn't tell that to Harold for a million pesos. I want him to come out swinging like he thinks he's gonna fight Mickey Walker. It'll be hard enough as it is."

The hall was almost full when the family entered and took their seats at ringside but Horace was not among them. The thought ran through Carl's head that if he were fighting, the nearness of so many interested relatives would make him nervous. Glancing at Harold, he saw him acknowledge the presence of the group with a wave of the hand then go about the business of limbering up in the same methodical manner as before.

The crowd was getting restless. "*Andamos á trompis*, let's box, someone shouted then, "On with the curtain raiser or throw out the boxers."

Ready for action now, Harold held out his hands for Quate to put on the eight-ounce gloves.

"Win or lose, you'll need fast fingers at the end," Quate said cryptically.

Carl's eyes widened in surprise when he saw that Quate had substituted ties, wider than the usual laces, and, after pulling them tight, he was tying them in bows instead of knotting them. Carl was about to ask why when the referee stepped in the ring and waved his hand for silence.

"Ladies and gentlemen, in this corner we have Young Joey, the pride of Datil, weighing in at a hundred fifteen and three-quarter pounds—"

Young Joey stepped forward and shook his gloved hands above his head in the traditional boxer's victory gesture while the crowd roared approval.

"And in this corner a boy, born in Silver City to be sure, but mostly raised in the gentle atmosphere of the mining town of Mogollon—" This drew laughter from the good-natured crowd—"that promising young boxer, Battling Bibo!" More roars of approval.

The referee mumbled his instructions to the boxers. When he finished Carl heard Young Joey say, "I'm going to wipe up the floor with you, Bibo." Harold's back was toward Carl but from previous experience he could have sworn that this remark would provoke absolutely no change of expression on Harold's face nor had the challenge forced a single audible word.

"Shake hands and come out fighting."

The moment Carl heard this order he forgot everything but the action. The first round was a jumble of feinting, dodging, and slipping punches on Harold's part as he tried to get in close enough to find his target. Young Joey's height and reach enabled him to land a number of blows but none of them were solid enough to slow down the swift-moving Harold. In the last few seconds Harold got in and under Joey's long arms and brought a right all the way up from the

126

floor that landed smack in Young Joey's middle, doubling him over. The clang of the bell and Joey's grunt of pain were simultaneous.

"Sponge off his face," Quate ordered as soon as Harold sat down. While Quate massaged Harold's legs he whispered to him, "Next round, as soon as the bell rings, leap up with a punch. That's the only way you can reach him."

The one-minute rest was over and the strident bong rang out again. Young Joey had barely moved an inch out of his corner when he was staggered by a tornado hurtling at him from across the ring. The surprise in Joey's blinking eyes changed to a daze as the round went on and Harold kept dealing out punishment. Carl's fists were clenched throughout and so were his teeth, to prevent himself from uttering forbidden words of encouragement, but under his breath he kept saying to himself, "Come on, Harold, you can do it. Come on, come on."

The packed hall came alive. People jumped to their feet to get a better look at the action and some of the ladies climbed onto their chairs. Cries of "Put him away, Bibo!" and "Stop the waltzing, Joey!" vied with thunder from the stamping heels of cowboy boots. Waves of applause rumbled through the hall as Harold landed one blow after another.

When the bell rang Carl noticed that Young Joey's second was holding a bottle of smelling salts to his nose in his corner.

"Okay, okay," Quate said. "He got the first round,

you took the second. You need the third now to get the decision. More of the same and keep your hands up high."

Harold started the third round with the same vigor, but Young Joey had acquired some vigor of his own and a little more know-how. He landed a solid left to Harold's jaw then, when Harold hesitated for a moment, he dealt him a clubbing blow at the back of the neck. Harold wobbled and Carl gnawed on his fist to keep from crying out. The crowd had no such restrictions and they immediately set up a cry of "Foul blow!"

These words got through to Harold. Suddenly his head cleared and he tore into his opponent with a series of body punches that buckled Young Joey's knees. When the bell rang Harold was still flailing, his face fire-red from a combination of anger and blows.

There was no wait for the decision. The referee grabbed Harold's arm and held it up bellowing, "The winner, Battling Bibo, the flying terror of Mogollon!"

The decision was followed by cheers and then the silver dollars began to spin through the air, landing inside the ring. While Young Joey's trainer was struggling to unlace his gloves, Harold pulled on the ends of the bow ties with his teeth, slipped off the gloves, tossed them to Quate, and began to scoop up silver cartwheels as fast as he could.

"Attaboy, Harold." Quate laughed. "Here's a purse

to put 'em in."

Harold caught the leather purse and had it stuffed full by the time Young Joey was able to free his fingers and start picking up the leftovers.

"Okay, boys, clear the ring. The main attraction's coming up."

"How'd I do, pop?" Harold asked as Paolo came up and put his arm around his son's shoulders.

"Great! I was proud of you all the way. You didn't use the short left hook enough when you got inside but, after all, that's the first time you've fought anybody that much taller. I don't think the kid meant to give you a rabbit punch. Because you're so much shorter, and he's not too hep at placing his punches, I believe it just happened to land that way."

"I don't think he meant to either," Harold said, "but in a way it was a good thing. It made me mad enough to slug a giant."

The main bout was on now and they began to make their way toward the rear of the hall. As they reached the door the frock-coated gambler, looking more than ever as though he'd just stepped off a Mississippi river boat, stopped in front of Harold and handed him a package.

"I never bet on a curtain raiser before in my life, but I had a hunch. Because of you, Bibo, I won two hundred bucks. Here's ten of 'em."

"That was big of him," Carl said as the gambler walked away.

"Don't give him too much credit for being soft-hearted," Quate said. "The way it goes is this. Harold brought him good luck. If he didn't do something back for Harold his luck might change. It's kinda like a charm. Paying off keeps bad luck away."

"You mean he's superstitious," Carl said.

"All right, you can call it that if you want to. I call it common sense."

The four ladies—Juana, Plácida, María, and Helen —had threaded their way through the crowd and now they surrounded Harold, kissing and congratulating him.

"Solomon, Leo, and Wilbert are staying for the main event," Juana explained as she looked with concern at a bruise on Harold's cheek that was rapidly turning into purple and green patchwork, "but we've had enough."

"I'm hungry," Harold said.

"I thought you would be so I fixed a special supper at home," Juana said. "Come along now and button up that bathrobe, Harold. The night air is chilly."

As they filed through the door Carl asked Helen, "What happened? Aren't you going to the dance?"

"When Leo and Wilbert decided to stay for the main bout my mother said it would be too late after, but it doesn't matter. We can play records while we have supper. It is much nicer to have the family together because soon the summer will be over and everybody will go away again."

"You didn't hear anything from Horace, did you?" Carl asked.

Helen shook her head sadly. "No. I wish he had been here too."

By the time supper was ready the main bout was over and the men had appeared. The moment they sat down at the table the group began to discuss the fight, analyzing and re-analyzing every move.

"After Harold got hit in the first round I only peeked through my fingers," Helen admitted. "I was afraid he'd get hurt bad."

"Do you know something," Aunt María said, "I feel as tired as if I had been in there fighting."

"It's the excitement," Solomon said with a yawn, "and the big supper on top of it. I worked as hard as you did, Harold, while you were in the ring, and at my age that's pretty strenuous exercise. Let's all turn in, folks."

Wasting no time at all, Harold got up from the table, mumbled, "G'night and thanks, everybody," and headed upstairs to his bunk. The women carried the dishes out to the kitchen and the men scattered—Leo and Solomon to make sure the store was securely locked, Wilbert to see that the horses and wagon were bedded down properly for the night, and Paolo to move his truck to the back of the store.

Quate began to repack his bucket of salves and liniments, wiping off the bottles and tightening the corks.

"Guess I'll go to bed," Carl said reluctantly, dead-tired but hating to see it end. "It sure was exciting."

"There, that's done." Quate put some wadded

newspapers over the top of the bucket and tied them down securely. "Now I can take off these clothes and get comfortable."

On a sudden impulse Carl asked, "Quate, how come the red *banda*? I never saw you wear one before."

Quate chuckled quietly, then he said, "It's like this. Remember the gambler? You got to do the right things to bring luck. Red *banda*, red shirt. I only wear them when my boxer has a fight. Red is the good luck Indian color. At the bottom of my bucket of salves and liniments I put a horseshoe that I begged off Señor Lavo. Even the bathrobe Harold wore, that belonged to Señor Paolo years ago when he used to box. You put all these things together and it makes good medicine."

7

A Cave Where Spirits Dwell

Harold, Paolo, and Quate were to leave early Sunday morning for Albuquerque. While they were getting ready to go Carl had a sudden inspiration. He ran to find Solomon and tell him what he wanted to do.

"That's a good idea. Ask Leo to open up the store for you," Solomon said. "You'd better hurry up because they're almost ready to leave."

When Carl found Leo and told him what he had in mind, Leo got the door unlocked in nothing flat and the two of them went over the merchandise in a hurry, trying to find the right thing.

Finally Carl said, "I see cousin Paolo's truck outside. This'll have to do."

Quate was about to clamber onto the rear of the truck when Carl rushed out to intercept him. "Wait a minute, Quate. I have something for you," Carl called. "I'm sorry I didn't have time to wrap it up."

He handed Quate the object he carried in his hand. It was a handsome, hand-woven, bright red belt with a big silver buckle engraved with Indian symbols. "Next time Harold fights," Carl paused, out of breath from his run, "wear this for luck along with the red *banda* and the red shirt."

Quate turned the belt over and over, not saying anything. It was hard for Carl to believe that Quate had finally run out of words. But he recovered quickly.

"Hold this for a minute." Quate thrust his bedroll at Carl, then, strapping the belt around his waist, he patted the buckle with both hands. "*Chico*, it's a perfect fit and I give you lots of thanks for it."

"I give you lots of thanks back," Carl said, "for the boxing lessons."

Quate made a throwaway gesture with one hand.

"It was nothing, the lessons, but tell me something." Cocking his head to one side, he looked at Carl with his bright black eyes. "Why did you give me the red belt? Was it—" then he chuckled—"superstition?"

Carl thought for a minute before he remembered the right answer. "No, common sense," he said, and they both laughed as Quate pumped his hand up and down before throwing the bedroll onto the truck and climbing aboard.

"Carl," Harold yelled as the motor started up, "we might get to see you again before you go home to San Francisco."

134

"I hope so," Carl called back. "So long, cousin Paolo! So long, Quate!"

The whole family had come out on the front porch to say farewell and they kept waving until the truck was a smudge of dust in the distance. As Carl walked back to the house he looked up and saw Juana coming down the path to meet him.

"Carlitos, my sisters have to leave this afternoon so you must pack up again if you want to go back to Ácoma. Oh my, it seems as though everybody comes at once and everybody leaves at once. We'll have Sunday dinner at twelve o'clock *en punto*, right on the dot. After dinner I want you and Wilbert to help Leo load the wagon. Get your things together. Now."

"Okay, mom."

As Carl climbed the stairs to the sleeping porch, Juana joined her sisters in the kitchen to start the task of preparing Sunday dinner. Carl saw that the three ladies were talking happily as they peeled and chopped, seasoned and tasted. The sisters, taken singly, were restrained and dignified, but Carl noticed that when they were together they chattered constantly in their native tongue, smiling and laughing as though they were girls again. As soon as another person entered the room they switched to Spanish or English for politeness' sake but it was obviously a joy for them to converse in their own Ácoma language. Everything in the house, including Juana's modern clothing, was exclaimed over, felt, and examined. Carl had caught a glimpse of the trio in his parents' bedroom yesterday afternoon before the fight. Plácida was trying on one of the tight-fitting cloche hats that were the style of the day. As she turned her head this way and that, her two thick black braids of hair switched back and forth. Quite aware of the humorous combination, she made droll faces at herself in the mirror while Juana and María giggled in appreciation.

My mother must miss them an awful lot, Carl thought. They have such good times together. He felt an increasing respect for the way Juana had accepted her life away from the pueblo.

Then he remembered his father telling how he, Solomon, had come to the United States at the age of sixteen. After a stormy voyage he landed in New York and worked in the East at any job he could find, scraping together the money for the long trek west. He followed camps erected for the construction of the Atlantic and Pacific railroad, running a little commissary for the workmen, supplying small items of food and clothing. It was a tedious journey, for he made barely enough in each place to replenish his supplies and move on. When he finally arrived in New Mexico to join his two older brothers, he hauled water, at first, for the workers building the Santa Fe railroad on a section of the Ácoma lands. It was here that he became acquainted with Martín Valle and his granddaughter Juana.

For Carl, coming to New Mexico, seeing the people and places had brought these stories alive. He was beginning to understand what Mr. Lummis had meant when he said, "I envy you, Carl, seeing it all for the first time."

Carl's packing was interrupted when Solomon poked his head in the doorway of the sleeping porch. "Are you going back to Ácoma this afternoon with the family, Carl?"

"I was planning to."

"All right, but don't get in the way. Natyati, the rainmakers' dance, starts next week. It's a very important ceremony. Do what you're told, don't ask questions, and you'll learn some interesting things."

As soon as Sunday dinner was over Carl and Wilbert began to pack up the wagon. It would return as heavily laden as it had arrived, for Juana and Solomon were as generous with their gift-giving as the family from Ácoma. Carl loaded a sack of coffee beans, bars of yellow laundry soap, bags of flour and sugar. These items that all had to be brought from outside the pueblo would be carefully stored for the long winter ahead when heavy snows could sever communications for weeks at a time.

Wilbert was hitching up the wagon when Carl had an inspiration for some additional gift-giving of his own.

"Helen," he called, "is there something special Horace likes that I could bring him from the store?"

"He really enjoys those long black licorice whips. Do you have any of those?"

"I think so. Wait a minute and I'll see."

Carl found a big glass jar of licorice behind the high wooden counter. Next to it was another jar of cinnamon balls, so he added some for good measure. He had just filled a bag when he felt a hand on his shoulder and heard his mother say, "You are taking a peace offering?"

"I guess you could call it that."

"Keep trying," Juana said in her gentle way. "It's the right thing to do."

Night had fallen by the time they reached the borders of the pueblo lands. It was a long journey by wagon back to Ácoma and for the last hour Carl's head had been nodding in rhythm with the slow sway. He was about to succumb and curl up in a corner when the sound of a horse's hoofs, thudding through the dark, jerked him awake.

"I wonder if it's Horace," he said aloud. "I wonder if he—" but his voice trailed off because Helen, sitting next to him, tapped his arm to get his attention, then put her finger to her lips to indicate silence.

Wilbert called out quickly, "Horace, is that you? We got started later than we planned. When I told you to take Zutu the other night I hope you made it back a lot faster than we did. Have you done all the things you said you had to do?"

The hoofbeats had stopped but there was a continuing silence as Horace registered the face-saving excuses for his desertion that Wilbert was trying to get across to protect him from grown-ups scolding.

Before Horace could speak Auntie Plácida said, "Horace, you should not have left the house without thanking Aunt Juana and Uncle Solomon."

"I told Wilbert to be sure and thank them for me. I guess he forgot." Horace said, turning Wilbert's cover-up to his own advantage.

"He did forget," Aunt María said sternly, "so you are both to blame."

Carl wanted to laugh at the quick way Horace had put Wilbert on the spot but Helen's pursed lips and shake of the head warned him to keep a straight face.

"Hey, wait a minute," Wilbert protested. "It's not my . . . well, okay. Next time we see the Bibos we'll both make, what do you call it . . .?"

"Apologies," Carl supplied.

"Right."

As soon as they arrived at the base of Ácoma the boys unloaded the wagon and packed the bags of groceries on the backs of the horses for the climb up the steep and narrow trail. It was hard for Carl to pick his way because clouds scudded across the sky obscuring the light from moon and stars. Ahead of him Aunt María walked, sure-footed among the rocks and ruts from a lifetime of practice. From time to time she glanced at the sky and as they reached the summit she said, "The *k'atsina*, the spirit rain-makers, are flying in from their home at Wenimats and are blowing the *shiwanna*, the storm clouds, across the moon. It is a good omen."

Unlike other nights at Ácoma, and although it was

late, Carl noticed that there were signs of activity. After the boys had carried the sacks of foodstuffs into the storeroom they took the horses to the corral behind the church. There were no lights anywhere but, as they returned, Carl saw several shadowy figures emerging from the head *estufa*. Although no one else was visible on the streets, spirals of smoke snaked up from several rooftops and there was a feeling of preparations taking place inside the homes.

The three boys walked in silence. Wilbert and Horace had not exchanged a word since their first encounter, and Carl wondered if Wilbert would speak to Horace about taking off with Zutu, his most prized possession. Saving face in front of adults was one thing, but Carl thought that Wilbert, with his strong sense of justice, would not let the incident pass. Carl did not envy Horace. The thought of being in bad with Wilbert bothered Carl more than anything else he could think of.

As they separated for the night, Horace said, "Wilbert, we have to get up early in the morning to practice for the rainmakers. The cacique says that our clan will dance the first two days."

"How early?"

"We must assemble at five o'clock."

"I'll meet you at four-thirty," Wilbert said. Then he added, "There's something I want to speak to you about first."

Horace nodded in agreement but made no comment. The rest of the walk was as silent as the first part had been.

It was a strange dream. The figure that moved through Carl's restless sleep stood with its back to him when it first appeared. It moved on two legs like a man but when it turned around its head was grotesque, shaped like a huge kettle upside down. Chalk white, with great round eyes circled in black, the mouth was a broad yellow protuberance that stuck out several inches. Around the neck of the weird creature was a fluffy collar of fox fur. Two feathers jutted out at an angle above what would have been an ear if the thing had possessed them.

It hovered above Carl for a period of time that had no beginning and no end, the staring eyes boring into him. Then slowly, the head detached itself from the body and floated through the room over to the wall. There it stopped, seeming to be pegged in place. A stream of smoke poured from the wide yellow mouth, gradually obscuring the whole head. Smoke oozed through the entire room, thick, gray and odorless, like fog. Then it dissipated to a yellowish haze.

Suddenly Carl sat up, making violent motions with his arms as though he were swimming. If he had been in a bed he would have fallen out, thumping himself awake in a hurry. But since his bed was a sheepskin on the floor, the return to consciousness was more of an effort. He rubbed his eyes hard and shook his

141

head to clear it. As soon as he knew where he was, he looked at the wall for the grotesque head but there was nothing hanging on the pegs but the family's ceremonial clothing and jewelry. No one was in the room besides himself. Misty light filtered through gray dawn as the sun struggled to begin its climb through the sky.

Carl saw that somebody had remembered him by the food that was laid out for his breakfast. But where was everyone so early in the day? Getting up, he yawned and stretched, then helped himself to a piece of fruit, noticing some little pots and brushes laid out by the fireplace. Munching on a slice of melon, he went over to examine them more closely. The four pots bore the remnants of brightly colored paints, but there was nothing nearby to disclose what they had been used for.

"Good morning, cousin-brother. Did you sleep well?" Helen entered the room carrying one of the big *tinajas* of water which she put down by the side of the fireplace.

Carl was about to ask what the paints were for when he remembered Solomon saying, don't ask questions. But Helen must have noticed his curiosity because she said, "You're wondering about the little pots. Those are for ceremonial paints we make for the rain dance. We use chimney soot mixed with white of egg for the black. We grind golden-colored rock for yellow, mix it with water, then blend it with yolk of egg. The red comes from clay at Ácoma, and

142

the blue-green from a rock called *mo'ock* that we find in the mountains to the west. All preparations for the rainmakers are going on now. At Ácoma this ceremony starts on the tenth of July every year. We are the only pueblo that has it on this date." As she spoke, Helen collected the pots and brushes, putting them neatly into a woven basket. "The men practice special songs and dances. The women grind corn, make bread, pottery, and all kinds of food. There is always a rabbit hunt too. That is why we were up so early today. Soon we will . . ."

Helen paused as though she were listening to something. Then Carl heard it too. Someone was going through the streets of the pueblo shouting words in Ácoma that he could not understand. Then the door opened and Horace ran in.

"The war chief is calling everyone to the rabbit hunt. Come, it is about to begin."

Helen put down her basket and started out but Carl hung back, not sure that he was supposed to go, but Horace motioned him along. "Carl, too. The cacique gave permission."

Outside, people were streaming out of their homes, climbing down ladders into the streets. In this event women participated as well as men and the object was to obtain as many rabbits as possible to make stews for the participants in the rainmakers' dance. All of the rituals, including the rabbit hunt, extended back so many centuries that no one knew when they had first been established. The crowd was pouring down the trails now onto the plains below Ácoma. At the foot of the big rock a number of horses and riders had gathered. Canvas-covered wagons were also being hitched up and people were climbing into them. The area where the hunt was to take place was a long distance out from the sky city and the wagons were stocked with canteens of water and food made up in individual packages for each to take with him when the hunt was on.

Wilbert rode up on Zutu as the family got into the wagon. Leaning down, he offered Carl his choice of a sling shot or throwing stick while Zutu pranced impatiently, eager to streak off to the hunting grounds.

"I guess I'll take the sling shot," Carl said dubiously. He had never killed anything and he wasn't sure that he wanted to. "I'm not real good with it but I'll give it a try."

Seeing his hesitation, Wilbert said, "Look at it this way. We kill rabbits only for food. If we do not kill them they get to be so many that they eat our crops and we starve during the winter. We do not hunt for sport. We hunt to live."

As soon as the wagons started up and the horses and riders galloped off, Carl turned to look back at Katzimo. The vivid colorings of sunrise had disappeared and the cool, silvery-green light of early morning enfolded the massive mesa, giving it a watery look as though it had just risen mysteriously from the sea. Carl thought that perhaps it had been born that way, millions of years ago.

144

Horace was driving the wagon and Carl, seated next to him, found himself saying, "Horace, have you ever climbed Katzimo?"

"No."

"Do you want to?"

"Why do you ask that?"

"Because I want to, more than anything."

There was no response but when Carl turned he caught a glimpse of an unfathomable look on Horace's thin face that made him seem as mysterious as Katzimo itself.

How many miles from Ácoma they traveled before stopping at the hunting grounds Carl did not know, but by the time they arrived the morning was well advanced. As Carl climbed out of the wagon to join the assembling crowd, the summer sun splattered heat across his cheekbones and bare arms in warning of the searing blasts to come later in the day. This was an area where Carl had never been before, far out in the vast Ácoma valley.

In the center of the group was the head war chief, Cutimiti, whose function was to start the ancient ritual. The war chief had already laid a small fire of grass and sticks and he was now sprinkling cornmeal in a circle around it. When that was completed he drew four lines across it, interesecting at the center. Then with flint and steel he kindled a spark and set off the fire. As he worked he sang a chant telling the story of how fire was discovered. When the smoke began to rise he arose, arms extended as he prayed.

146

"Sun hunter, I wish you to help me today. Make many cottontails and jack rabbits to come together here."

When the sacred fire was burning strongly the war chief selected several men as leaders of the hunt and, with a shout of "*hai-ko*," sent them running in different directions. Then he sent two more, and two more after that, until all assembled were running in divergent lines, taking off from the holy fire which served as the base of an ever-widening V. At a certain point, decided upon in advance, the two leading runners turned and started running toward each other until they met. All of the hunters, male and female, were now strung out along this extensive triangle and now the hunt began, with the rabbits enclosed within a human trap that moved steadily inward until all the hunters converged, laden with the kill.

When the war chief indicated the order of the runners Carl had become separated from the family, and at the start of the hunt he found himself with strangers who soon disappeared among the scrub cedar and piñon trees. The countryside here was a rough rocky area spotted with sandy gulleys and boulders that the winds of time had sculptured into strange shapes. Carl heard voices in the distance and caught a glimpse of a throwing stick hurtling through the air.

Trudging along, Carl pursued occasional flickers that turned out to be lizards interrupted in their sunbathing. Suddenly something tawny streaked by him with a brief hoarse bark. It was a coyote forced to escape from his territorial hunting grounds, yielding his natural prey temporarily to man. In the next instant a speck, floating above Carl in the sky, plummeted down and with a spread of wings wheeled gracefully and became a hawk looking for his share of the fleeing rabbits.

After this encounter with wild life, Carl walked on for what seemed like miles without catching sight of a single cottontail. Once he was startled to a stop by a slithering movement near one of the misshapen boulders. Diamondback rattlers with heads as big as a man's fist were a grim reality in this part of the world, especially in the heat of the summer months. After this scare he decided to seek company and paused, listening for sounds of activity so he would know which direction to take. The intensity of the silence matched the intensity of the noonday sun directly overhead.

"Hello," he called, but not so much as an echo broke the stillness. Turning around slowly, he scanned the countryside for some identifying landmark. Where was the boulder he had noticed before, shaped like a miniature castle? Seeing a rock in the distance, he walked toward it, trying to distinguish its outlines through the mirage-like shimmers of heat. But as he drew nearer he saw that this one resembled a flatiron. He stopped again, glancing in one direction, then another. Once more he called out.

"Hello, there! I'm lost! I'm Carl Bibo."

He thought he heard footsteps behind him and

spun around to greet his rescuer. It was only the
wind exhaling a sudden breath that sent a whirl of
grit into his face. There was no one there. There was
no one anywhere as far as he could see over the plains.
As he rubbed his smarting eyes he fought against the
fear that gripped him.

Drenched with perspiration, he took a swig at his
water bottle. There was not much left in it. His heart
began to pound and the oven-like wind blew up
again, drying his cheeks and lips until his skin felt as
parched as the corn husks wrapped around the lunch
that Aunt Plácida had given him. He had put the
packet inside his shirt for safekeeping. It was still
there but he had no appetite for food. It was liquid
that he craved but he dared not drink his last few
ounces of water, in case he might be in greater need
of it later.

"Don't panic," he said aloud. The first thing was to
get out of the sun, but how? To his left was a small
mesa that seemed not too far away, but Carl had been
in this clear air long enough to know that an object
that looked close could be countless miles away.
There was really no choice though. He began to walk.

Time became a throbbing pulse that beat like a
clock in the top of his head. The day was a vast desert
set high in a sky burning white with heat that
shriveled every living thing. The sun changed to fever
that scorched one minute and sent shivers of cold
down his spine the next. Water was a cool blue lake
just ahead dissolving into fiery dust the moment he

set his feet in it. Shade lay in the inviting purple shadows cast by the cliffs of a mesa he never reached. Crying was something forbidden except, except . . .

Carl walked right into it. Placing both palms against its rough stone sides, he felt tears run down his cheeks. Now that he had reached the mesa he might survive long enough for them to find him. Exhausted, he sank down onto the rubbly talus and stretched out in the shade cast by the overhang of the flat-topped rock above him. Though his eyes were closed, silvery zigzags danced before him with a strange dizzying effect like lightning in the dark. His head spun, then his body became weightless, and he left it behind as he was sucked down a long, black tunnel.

When he awoke he reached for the water bottle and, half-dazed, drained the last drops, wincing from the pain of cracked lips and blistered skin. The few ounces of liquid only increased his thirst and he searched the lengthening shadows for any plant that might contain moisture. There was nothing but scrub cedar. He got to his feet shakily and, with all his strength, sent cry after cry out into the valley, listening after each shout for a reply, but it was as though there was no one left on earth but himself.

Sitting down, he stared at the ground disconsolately. He told himself that they would find him soon, and reason told him to stay right where he was, not to risk going out into the desert again, especially with night coming on. Despite his discomfort he knew that he wouldn't die of thirst, at least for a long time, nor hunger either. The packet of food was still inside his shirt. It was the inactivity, not being able to do anything to help himself that made him think of foolish alternatives. Then it struck him. He realized that there was something he could do to find out his location, but it had to be done before sunset. Getting to his feet, he began to circle the mesa. It was not very big around, not even a quarter of the size of Ácoma, but he thought it was high enough to serve his purpose. The only way he could tell for sure was to climb it.

Tearing open the food package, he chewed on some jerky to give him strength. He was so thirsty that it was hard to swallow the dry crispy meat, but he knew from scouting that salt was good for heat fatigue. As he ate he slowly searched the sides of the mesa with his eyes, looking for a likely place to try an ascent. Like Ácoma, there were many spots that offered a starting point, went up a few feet with possible toe and handholds, then changed into smooth rock impossible to scale.

He began circling the mesa again, inspecting every cranny, every niche. Suddenly he stopped, afraid to believe his luck. Here was an ascent that led up to a ledge that was almost at the top. The indentations in the rock were so regular that they could have been man-made. It was hard to tell from here whether these same convenient toeholds continued above the ledge and all the way to the top. Details were lost in shadows. He began to climb. If he could not go all the way he could always come back down again.

It would have been an easy climb except that exhaustion overcame him long before he reached the ledge. The gulping breaths of air that he took made a wheezing animal-like sound in his throat and the rapid beat of his heart pounded everything into blackness before his eyes. For one agonizing second he felt sandstone crumble beneath his fingers and knew that if he teetered backward a fraction of an inch he would be hurtled onto the jagged rocks below. He dug down hard and held fast for that necessary moment.

Praying with all his might to reach the ledge, he moved, inch by inch, the massive weights that had become his arms and legs. When he flopped over onto the safety of the ledge he lay there on his back, spread-eagled as though he had been dropped from the sky. He became aware that cool drafts of air were pouring over his body, many degrees colder than the desert temperature. Looking over his shoulder, he saw a narrow opening in the rock, just wide enough for a man to squeeze through, behind it inky darkness. Was there a cave inside? He would investigate later after he came down from the summit.

Struggling to his feet again, he reached up and probed the rock that was in shadows above him. The indentations were there. It was only a short way to the top. Willing his leaden body to move, he grasped the projection of rock overhead. In a few seconds he was on the summit, standing straight, no longer tired. He could see over the entire valley. There was Katzimo in the distance, aflame with the ruddy sunset, beside it the smaller rock that was Ácoma. Katzimo looked like a beacon lighting the way home, and it seemed to Carl that the great mesa possessed knowledge of his plight and that it reached out to meet his needs. If he wasn't found tonight he knew now what direction to take to reach safety tomorrow morning.

By the time he clambered down to the ledge again the evening star was visible in the sky but there was still enough light to locate the opening in the rock. Turning sideways, he passed into the darkened interior of a cave. There was a dramatic drop in temperature that changed his soaking shirt into a cool poultice against his skin. At first he could see nothing, then, as his eyes adjusted, he saw the outlines of a familiar object almost within reach. He touched it with his fingers. There were drops of moisture on the satiny surface. Raising the *tinaja* to his lips, he drank deeply of the life-saving water. As he replaced the jug in its corner he noticed four small piles of corn on the floor of the cave. Each pile was of a different color—yellow, blue, red, and black—and there were four feather-tufted prayer sticks, their tips worked into the sandstone so that they stood upright.

This is a sacred place, a praying place, Carl thought. Probably a *tinaja* of water was kept here at all times and the toeholds and fingerholds were made by man centuries ago. In the recess of the cave he could barely discern some shadowy masses that resembled seated figures. He took a step toward them when, suddenly, he was in utter darkness as though night had been ordered to descend upon one whose curiosity might get out of bounds. He turned abruptly, feeling a force directing him back toward the entrance of the cave. At the same moment he had an impulse to say his Indian name aloud.

"Kai-stee-zee," he said in a low voice. The echoes bounced back at him from all sides of the cave, the syllables overlapping until there was a sibilant, unending whisper as of many voices repeating over and over, "Kai-stee-zee, Kai-kai-stee-zee-zee-zee." As the echo trailed off, the knowledge came to him that he must get outside on the ledge as quickly as possible. Stretching out his arms in the dark, his fingers found the narrow opening. As he passed through he heard another sound.

"Carl? Carl Bibo, where are you?" called through the night.

"I'm here," he shouted, "up on the ledge. Where are you?"

"Down below. I've got a lantern. Stay there until I light it." A flame flickered through the dark and someone at the foot of the mesa held up a lantern. "Can you see to climb down now?"

"Pretty well. Come in a little closer. Then I think I can make it."

Cautiously he lowered himself, more by instinct than by sight, for the sky was cloudy, obscuring the

154

usually bright light of moon and stars. He felt a firm hand on his elbow guiding him for the last few feet.

"You can't have any broken bones or you wouldn't be able to climb down like that." It was Wilbert, holding the lantern aloft, scrutinizing Carl carefully. The frown on his face changed to a smile as he completed the inspection. "You're dirty, that's all. You didn't get hurt. What happened?"

The words tumbled out as Carl explained. While he spoke, Wilbert swung the lantern back and forth as a signal to the other searchers. Soon there was the sound of galloping hoofs. The high-pitched cries of the riders competed with the shrill whinnying of the horses in ear-piercing discord.

"How long have you been looking for me?" Carl asked.

"All afternoon, going round and round the place where we held the rabbit hunt."

"How did you know where to find me?"

"When we finally rode back to Ácoma and reported your disappearance to the chief, he said, "Return to the ground where you held the rabbit hunt and ride a few miles through the land where the *chuski* live, the coyotes. You will find a small mesa and there you will find Carl too.""

"But how did he know?" Carl asked.

Before he could receive an answer he and Wilbert were surrounded by horses and riders. In a few moments they were securely mounted on Zutu, heading home to Ácoma.

8

The *K'atsina* Fight Back

Since Carl had suffered no ill effects from his adventures in the cave, the family, along with the rest of the pueblo at Ácoma, continued preparations for the important ceremonial of Natyati, the rainmakers' dance. Carl eagerly assisted in whatever jobs he was asked to do and, though most of the requests came from the women and might have been considered the female division of labor, it was all new to Carl and he carried out his chores with interest.

He lugged endless *tinajas* of water from the big reservoir to Aunt Plácida's house. He watched the nimble fingers of Plácida and Helen dipping into bowls of water to moisten coils of clay before molding them into ceremonial dishes and cooking vessels. After these were fired they would be used in preparing special food for the dancers. The potter's wheel was unknown to the people of Ácoma in prehistoric times but once it became known it was still never used. Their pottery was truly handmade.

Carl saw the round loaves of delicious bread that he

ate every morning being removed from adobe ovens shaped like beehives. These outdoor ovens were located on the flat roofs of the second story of most of the houses at Ácoma. The cedar wood placed in the oven was allowed to burn down to hot coals. These coals were then scraped out and the yeast dough, in pottery bowls, thrust inside. A rock slab over the opening served as a door. The texture and flavor that resulted from this unusual method was unlike any other that Carl had ever tasted.

Great pots of rabbit stew began to simmer and the savory odor of spicy chiles and wild herbs filled the air. Quantities of melons, grapes, oranges, peaches, and plums were assembled and the rasp of *metates*, grinding corn into meal, became background music that accompanied the many activities taking place from dawn until sunset.

Wilbert explained to Carl that the ceremonies lasted four days, even if rain began on the very first day, and that only the males of the tribe participated in the dancing. In the *estufas* the headmen repainted and repaired, if necessary, the ancient *k'atsina* masks, made of buffalo hide or deerskin, that represented the spirit rain gods. *K'atsina* dolls were carved of wood, then painted and decorated with feathers and flowers. These dolls were given to the children by masked dancers during the ceremony and were highly prized by the young. The cacique, the war chiefs, and the medicine men attended to the numerous religious details that must be scrupulously observed. Wilbert

pointed out that nothing could be omitted for fear of ruining the medicine that would bring the much-needed rain for crops upon which the very lives of his people depended during the winter months.

Although Wilbert and Horace were allowed to remain at their homes during the day before the ceremonies began, they could not partake of any food or drink at supper. Fasting, starting before sundown, was part of the ritual for the dancers. After the evening meal at Aunt Plácida's, Wilbert came by to pick up Horace. Carl walked down the street with his cousins and said good-bye to them a little wistfully as they entered the *estufa* where they would join the other dancers of their clan and pass the night in preparations for the rites that began at sunrise. He would have liked to share in all of the observances made by the males of the tribe but he knew that this was impossible since he had not been brought up in the religion of the Ácomas. The streets were very quiet. Somewhere out on the plains a coyote howled, but not one of the numerous dogs in the pueblo sent up even a yelp in reply. A hush lay over the sky city and it seemed to deepen with each passing moment.

Carl was reluctant to go indoors, so he turned toward the church, walked down the road to the edge of the mesa, and looked out to where Katzimo lay brooding in the night. He could see the outline of the enchanted mesa clearly because the moon was riding high now, its brilliance enhanced by myriads of stars. If there was a trace of rain in the heavens it was not visible to anyone but the gods themselves. From the evidence before Carl's eyes it was hard to believe that the dancers could pull moisture out of that cloudless sky. Reason told him that it couldn't happen, but instinct told him something else. His experience in the cave had not frightened him but he had been awed by the forces around him and by the way the cacique had known where to find him. He hadn't asked for further explanation because his father had told him not to ask questions, and he also felt that whatever Lorenao Watshm Pino wanted him to know he would tell him. Turning toward home, he walked slowly back through the deserted streets. The air was filled with mysteries that were a part of nature that Carl did not fully understand.

When Carl returned to Aunt Plácida's, he met his uncles, Cipriano and Edward, for the first time.

As Uncle Cipriano shook hands with Carl he explained, "We are sorry for not coming to see you sooner, Carl. Your Uncle Edward wants very much to finish his house before the first snows fall. Here, at Ácoma, it is always hard work to make ze-wee-tai, mother nature, help us to grow our crops or build our shelters."

"Did you find water yet?" Carl asked.

It was Uncle Edward who replied. "Ten times we have dug, ten times we have hit rock. This morning, after days and days of digging in this new place, the same thing happened. I was so angry that I grabbed my axe and, swinging with all my strength, I smashed the solid rock as hard as though I was chopping off the head of a rattlesnake. Suddenly my moccasins were soaking wet. I couldn't believe my eyes. I thought maybe the *k'atsina* had started sending the rain down already before the Natyati began. Because of the blow I had struck, water was coming out. I made my hands into a cup and tasted it. It was real, it was good. At once I gave thanks, not only to the *k'atsina* but to Cipriano, my brother-in-law, who has helped me for such a long time. We came only to tell the good news to María and Plácida and to say hello to you, Carl. In a few minutes we go back and at first light tomorrow we start building the house."

Next morning Carl was out on the rooftop before anyone else appeared. As soon as the black night clouds smoldered with the fire of approaching dawn, the doors to the *estufas* opened and the *k'atsina* dancers began to emerge. Suddenly, as though a bell had rung, every rooftop in Ácoma was thronged with people. For a few minutes the crowd was hushed as though in silent prayer, then little sounds peppered the quiet, gradually gathering to a mass murmur that quickly subsided into the normal hum of the pueblo. Carl felt a surge of excitement mixed with pride that Wilbert and Horace were among the imposing figures that were now spilling down the ladders and into the street. The masks were wondrous to behold. Some represented women with long hair and faces painted red, yellow, green, or white. These *k'atsina* carried

161

large gourds which they rattled in a slow starting rhythm. Other masks were fashioned like birds and were adorned with feathers and beaks. Helen joined Carl on the rooftop and suddenly Carl exclaimed, "Look at that one! It's the head I thought I saw in a dream, but it's real after all." The chalk-white face, with great round eyes circled in black, wobbled by.

Laughing at Carl's expression, Helen explained, "That's Wai'oca, the duck. Someone probably took him out of the storeroom when you were sleeping to bring him to the *estufa* for repairs. Do you see the *k'atsina* with the white faces and the crosses on their foreheads?"

"Yes, I do. What are they carrying in those little bowls?"

"The bowls are filled with ashes and if any spectators come too close to the dancers then the *mictcaikoros* —that's what they're called—are supposed to throw ashes into their eyes."

There were about forty *k'atsina* dancers in all. During the course of the morning they followed a definite route, dancing in eight different locations around the surface of the big rock of Ácoma. As the hours passed, the beat of the *tombé* and the rattling of the gourds grew faster and faster. Carl was amazed by the endurance of the dancers. It was the hottest day yet that he had experienced at the pueblo. From beneath the heavy masks, sweat streamed down bare torsos. Soon the dancing skirts worn by the men were streaked with weird rainbows from the varicolored

162

paints they used on their bodies and arms. The morning ceremonial ended at noon behind the church. The men were served food, then they practiced a few chants and once more began the exhausting dance that took them to the eight points on the surface of the pueblo.

At intervals during the day, Carl scanned the sky, looking for signs of the much-needed rain. Nothing marred the glaring blue bowl. Not the tiniest shred of a cloud caused the fierce golden eye of the sun to blink even once.

"It still doesn't look a bit like rain," Carl said to Helen as he helped her take some empty pots up the ladder.

"It will," Helen said confidently.

"Do you really believe that?"

"Of course."

"I believe it too, but I wish it would hurry."

"You must learn patience, cousin-brother," Helen said primly.

Just before sunset the *k'atsina* entered the plaza where the cacique and the war chiefs awaited them for the closing rituals of the day. In back of the houses on the north side of the plaza the women of the pueblo had hidden gifts of food and *k'atsina* dolls. When all the dancers were assembled, the head *k'atsina* left the group and slowly approached the cacique. With arms extended, he bowed respectfully before the elder of the tribe. Draped in his ceremonial blanket, Lorenao Watshm Pino returned the salute with unhurried dignity. The dancers broke ranks and went to get the hidden gifts which they piled before the cacique in the plaza.

All the people of the pueblo were assembled, the youngsters clinging to their mother's skirts, round-eyed with anticipation as they saw the pile of gifts grow. When all the *k'atsina* had returned, they danced and chanted briefly, then they began to distribute the gifts, tossing some into the crowd, handing dolls to the children.

Freed from restraint, the children ran and shouted with delight, gathering presents. There were some tugs of war but no fighting, and Carl noticed many instances where bigger and faster youngsters shared with the little ones whose tears had begun to fall. When all gifts were distributed the *k'atsina* assembled once more and danced their way out of the plaza, back to the *estufas*, ending the day's ceremonies.

The second day the ritual was repeated. Carl could detect no change in enthusiasm among either the dancers or the people of the pueblo, nor was any concern expressed at clear skies and lack of rain. Taking a cue from Helen, Carl didn't comment on stubborn clouds that wouldn't appear. When he scanned the sky he did it furtively, not wanting anyone to catch him at it. At the end of the second day the group of dancers to which Wilbert and Horace belonged would end their part in the Natyati and yield to the next group, who would carry to completion the four-day period. The only change in the rites on the second day was the giving of prayer sticks by the cacique to the dancers.

The *hachamoni* had been carved by the men themselves as part of their duties. At sunset, the head dancer accepted the basket of prayer sticks from the chief, then all of the *k'atsina*, still wearing their masks, walked down the trail to the southern section of the mesa where the great reservoir lay. Each man picked out his own prayer stick and prayed with it. It was appropriate that the ritual should end here, for rain was not only necessary for the crops but to refill the reservoirs, which were the main source of water supply for the "city in the sky."

That evening Horace and Wilbert returned home to sleep. Carl was waiting impatiently outside the house for his cousins. Although he had watched with great interest for the last two days, and had willingly done whatever was asked of him, he had missed the companionship of the boys. As soon as he saw them he climbed down the ladder to meet them.

"It was great," Carl said, "the dances, the chants, everything."

"We did our best, cousin-brother, even though we didn't bring the rain yet," Wilbert said. He looked fresh and full of energy, but Horace's thin face was worn. "I have to take care of Zutu now," Wilbert said. "I haven't seen him for two days. I'll see you tomorrow morning."

Carl watched Wilbert walk off down the street, then he said to Horace, "Do you think the rain will come tomorrow?"

"It will never come as long as you're here."

"What do you mean by that?"

"You ruined it for our dancers because you're an Anglo and Anglos shouldn't be allowed."

For a moment Carl was so angry he couldn't speak. His fists clenched and with a great effort he kept his arms at his sides. So strong was his desire to land a blow on that accusing face in front of him that he took several steps backward, knowing that he had to put distance between himself and Horace. Finally he said, his voice shaking, "You purified your body by fasting. Why didn't you clean out your mind, get some of the hate out of it?"

"Don't make fun of our religion."

"You're the one who's making fun of it. If you really had faith then you'd believe that nobody from outside could possibly have any effect."

"I can't fight you now," Horace muttered, "because that might hurt the medicine we've made to bring the rain, but I'll beat you up as soon as this is over."

"Try it. I've been waiting for you. Just try it."

"Go away," Horace said, "and stay away. We don't want you here."

The gulp of air Carl took as he fought back the tears was as audible as a sob in the stillness of the night. He began to run without taking heed of the direction. Suddenly the graveyard and church loomed up before him, eerie in the last moments of twilight, bleak and unwelcoming in cold shades of gray. Afraid

166

that someone might pass by and see him if he stopped, Carl ran around the back of the church and threw himself on the ground. Trembling with the effort of trying to keep his tears under control, he heard a neigh and then a whinny, and realized that his entrance had disturbed the horses tethered there. With a sinking heart he heard a familiar voice behind him.

"What's up, Carl? You ran in here as though *k'anadyaiya,* the evil spirits, were after you."

Although he trusted and respected Wilbert, Carl could not confide in him. He knew he couldn't explain without crying, so he mumbled, "I felt like running, that's all. I slipped and fell when I got in here."

"Okay, come say hello to Zutu. He's been lonesome."

Carl was grateful that it was really dark now and that Wilbert couldn't see the expression on his face. Obediently he followed along. As he rubbed Zutu's shaggy mane he began to regain his composure and he felt he could speak without having his voice break.

"Listen, Wilbert, have you got an extra sheepskin or a blanket I could borrow? I think I'll sleep out tonight."

"You can come to my house if you want."

"I—thanks, but—well, I think I'd rather not."

"Tell you what, do you think you can handle Zutu?"

"Sure I do."

"He needs some exercise and if you have him along you won't get lost. Wherever you end up for the night it won't matter. Tomorrow morning you just say to him, 'Home, Zutu. Back to Ácoma,' and he'll bring you home straightaway."

"That would be neat."

"I've got a blanket right over here and there's jerky and dried peaches in the saddle bag. You sure you don't want to go home with me?"

"I'm sure. I'll take good care of Zutu."

Wilbert laughed. "It'll be the other way round. Zutu'll take good care of you. What about Aunt Plácida? She'll be worried."

"Will you tell her I won't be back tonight?"

"As soon as I leave here."

"Thanks a lot."

Wilbert helped Carl get the things together. After Carl had mounted the pony, Wilbert stood there for a moment patting Zutu's flank. "You're sure you want to do this? You haven't changed your mind?"

"I have to do it," Carl said.

Wilbert nodded, then waved good-bye as the pony started slowly down the trail. Carl waved back, stopped for a moment, then called out, "Don't worry if I don't come back until day after tomorrow." He prodded the pony into a canter. He wanted to put distance between himself and Wilbert so that if his cousin had any objections to a longer stay he wouldn't be able to hear them. If Horace really believed that his presence kept the rain from coming, then it might help if he stayed away until after the Natyati was over.

As soon as Zutu got onto the plain, Carl could feel

the pony's eagerness to be off. The horse had been confined for several days, as had his rider. Both were young, strong, and needed to expend energy. Leaning over, Carl whispered into Zutu's ear, "I'm not the greatest rider in the world but I trust you. Let's go, Zutu."

Zutu's ears twitched and he began a slow trot that gradually picked up a little speed. It was as though he was testing his rider, feeling Carl's muscular reaction to a gradual acceleration. It felt right to Carl. His confidence in himself and Zutu increased. Zutu caught the response, eased into a gallop, and suddenly it seemed to Carl that the animal became an extension of his own body. Now Zutu took off with great leaping strides and Carl experienced an exhilaration he had never known before. In his book of Greek mythology there was a picture of a centaur, a creature half man and half horse. It had happened to him. Boy and pony were one.

How long they sped on through the night Carl didn't know. He ceased to think. There was only the wonderful freedom of it all. At times they seemed detached from the earth itself; at other times they were part of the earth, with roots running along below the surface. When Zutu, using his own brand of horse-sense, finally stopped, it was at the little settlement of Ácomita. Carl had never been there before but he recognized, from Helen's description, that this was where she lived during the winter. In the bright moonlight he saw the tiny church she had told him about, where

169

classes were held for the pueblo children, and there was the little store where a few supplies could be bought. Ácomita was deserted now. All inhabitants were on the big rock for the *k'atsina* ceremonies. Zutu, familiar with the area, went directly to a water trough at the side of a lean-to filled with fodder. It was the perfect place to bed down for the night. Carl laughed aloud as he unbuckled the girth and swung the saddle off Zutu's back.

"This is a good place to bring a tenderfoot, Zutu, but if we stay out tomorrow night it won't be at Ácomita. We're going to ride a long way." Zutu rolled his eyes but didn't comment. Instead, he began munching fodder in a business-like way, as though he were storing it up for an uncertain future.

Carl awoke with the dawn. The first thing he did when he opened his eyes was to study the pearly gray skies for signs of rain. At first he was hopeful, but when the night sky had completely yielded to daylight he saw the same unbroken clarity that had gone before. Zutu nuzzled him to his feet and he felt again the eagerness in the pony to be off and running—but with a difference. They had tried each other, worked together, harmonized, and now they were ready to go without worrying about the outcome.

Whistling a little tune as he prepared for the day's journey, Carl noticed an adobe house down the road. The Acoma people sliced their lamb or deer meat paper-thin, then hung it out on lines to let the sun and mountain air do the drying. The yard of this house was strung with lines of meat, and Carl decided to take along an extra supply in his saddle bag. He would find out later who the owners were and tell them what he had done. He had just gathered half a dozen pieces when he remembered that his uncles, Cipriano and Edward, could be somewhere in the vicinity working on their housebuilding. He didn't want to run into them and have to make explanations so he hurried back to the lean-to. It didn't take long to put his gear together, and the lavender shadows of early morning had scarcely lifted when horse and boy were on their way again.

Outside Ácomita was the fertile bottomland of Blue Water Creek, the farming area for the whole pueblo. Carl rode through rippling wheat and corn fields, passed ripening melons growing heavy on the vines, red chiles, pinto beans, and peach orchards. This was the breadbasket of the pueblo, the reason why rain was so badly needed. As the morning wore on the countryside began to change. Soon they were in a rough area dotted with scrub cedar, piñon trees, and cactus. Zutu's pace slowed as he picked his way around boulders, sometimes paused to test ground when rock crumbled beneath his hoofs. At one point he came to a complete stop, reared, and changed direction at the sight of a huge diamondback rattler lying motionless and almost invisible along the cre- vasse of a black lava bed.

Carl hoped to reach shade by noon so that they

171

could avoid the blistering sun for a few hours. The territory they were in right now looked unpromising for an afternoon's siesta and he began to wonder if Zutu was lost.

"Zutu," he said aloud, "we need shelter from the sun. Can you find a place for us to stop?"

In answer, Carl felt the pull of muscles beneath him as the strong little pony began to ascend what looked like a man-made trail or, perhaps, a deer run, leading away from the rocky country and up the side of a mound. When they reached the crest Carl looked down on a cluster of half a dozen piñon trees that were larger and leafier than those he had seen before. In a few minutes he and Zutu were in a shaded area. The small grove of trees was explained because a spring bubbled up from the ground, feeble but more magnificent to Carl at that moment than the mightiest river.

He spent the next few hours eating, dozing, and whittling away at some sticks he found nearby. While he worked he hummed or whistled, not thinking of anything, glad to be comfortable. Nothing disturbed the peace, certainly not a raindrop. Rain; he stopped whittling. Walking to the edge of his tree shelter, he looked out at the sky. It was unchanged. Hot speckles of sunshine dappled his face and arms through the leaves above, fiery reminders that, so far, the efforts of the Natyati had been in vain. In one hand he still held the knife he'd been whittling with, in the other the twig. As he retreated back into the shade he

172

realized that, without meaning to, his carving resembled a prayer stick.

"Maybe I should make one for the *k'atsina*," he said aloud. He knew that the stick he had just made wouldn't do, because he had observed at Ácoma that the *hachamoni* were always fashioned of green wood cut from a living tree. Reaching up, he hacked off a piece of piñon about eight inches long. Then he sat down on the ground, tailor-fashion, and went about his work, remembering as best he could some of the shapes and designs he had seen. He knew that the stick should be painted and that feathers should be tied around one end, but he had no way of doing this right now. He hoped the *k'atsina* would forgive the omissions and that the medicine of the prayer stick would be just as powerful without them.

When the *hachamoni* was completed, the afternoon was well advanced and it was time to move along again. He put the stick in his pocket. He would wait until he saw a suitable place to put it. In the cranny of a rock or on a ledge was where they were placed at Ácoma. He would try to find something similar. When Carl mounted Zutu again, he said, "Okay, Zutu, let's see something different." He was determined to spend the night out and all of the next day, if necessary. He didn't want to give Horace any reason for accusing him of preventing rain in these last two days of the dance.

The second night Carl was not nearly as much at ease as he had been the first. He knew that if he had not had the companionship of the horse he would have been really scared. They rode for so long across the darkening plain that Carl lost track of time completely. He had no idea where he was, only the sure knowledge that he had never been there before. The night was black, starless, indifferent. Zutu seemed keyed-up and edgy, rather than high-spirited as he usually was, and he communicated this tension to Carl. When Carl whispered, "Zutu, it's time to stop for the night," the pony went on running, not slackening speed, nor changing direction. Carl didn't lose faith in him, but tonight he knew he was riding a horse, that he was an inexperienced rider, and that he was rapidly becoming exhausted. The blending of boy and beast that had happened the night before was gone.

At a point when Carl was ready to stop, no matter where they were, he felt the familiar pull as the horse began an ascent. It was a steep one; the animal quivered with exertion. Carl would have dismounted to lighten Zutu's load except that he could see nothing but huge black masses looming up on either side. He was aware that Zutu knew all of this territory and that instinct would keep the pony surefooted where he, Carl, in his weariness, might stumble and fall. He hung on, rocking in the saddle with the bumpy ride, chilled to the bone from the drop in temperature of the desert night. He longed for a fire, hot food, familiar faces around him. What was he doing here so far from home, fighting hostility, trying to understand things that were really beyond him? Not only was the ground beneath him strange, but the people, their customs, the whole way of life. Maybe Horace was doing him a favor when he told him to go away. Maybe he was only being honest when he said, "We don't want you here."

Carl had been tired for hours but now the negative quality of his thoughts finished him off. The moment Zutu stopped, he slid off the horse, did only what was absolutely necessary to prepare himself and the animal for the night, then, rolling up in his blanket, he lay down on the ground with the lumpy saddle bag beneath his head and fell into the drugged sleep of total exhaustion.

Next morning every muscle in his body ached as he groaned himself awake. He didn't know how he felt; he was still too numb from lying for hours in the same cramped position. As he struggled to his feet, he forgot everything but the sight that greeted him. Zutu had carried him to the top of a cliff from where he could see the sweep of the wonderland called Ácoma, lying bleached white before him in the early morning sun. Below him was an enormous bridge of natural stone across which a hundred men could file without crowding. It looked as though it had been formed by an ancient river that had found a crack through the cliffs and, through countless centuries, had enlarged this opening until its surging waters eroded the rock into a massive arch of stone. Beneath the bridge, pinnacles and crags jutted up from the plains. As the light changed, they seemed to undulate, assuming different forms, becoming living sculpture wrought by giants. Katzimo, hardly showing in the distance, was smudged by hazy veils of night mist not yet stripped away by the revealing hand of Pa-yat-ya-ma, sun-father.

Carl didn't know how long he stood there, but gradually he became aware that this day was going to be as implacably bright and clear as those that had gone before. His hand went to the pocket of his shirt. The prayer stick was still there. He began to walk the top of the cliff, peering over the side, looking for a ledge. Finally he saw one that was wide enough, but it was far below. Stretching out full length, he took aim. The stick landed at the very edge, teetered for a second, then steadied itself, half protruding over the side.

"*K'atsina*, bring rain," Carl murmured.

By late afternoon Carl and Zutu had made their way to the base of Katzimo. From here it was not far to Ácoma and Carl knew that, rain or no rain, he would have to return to the pueblo by sunset or his aunts would be worried about him. They might even send out a search party again, which would cause trouble and embarrassment to everyone and make Horace scorn him even more. He had wedged himself into a shady cleft of the enchanted mesa, which went deep into the side of the huge stone table. The far recesses behind him, which he had not explored, were as black as jet. He was tempted to go in further, if only to while away the time, but something kept him back. He was tired and tense and he knew it could be his imagination, but it seemed to him that Katzimo held him off. Zutu was not at ease either. The pony moved restlessly back and forth, and Carl picked up the halter and held it slack in his hand in case Zutu might decide to run away.

The afternoon grew hotter and stickier as the sun began to descend. Carl dozed occasionally, but each time he did, the discomfort of his clothes, wringing wet from perspiration and plastered against his body like a strait jacket, twitched him awake. The last time his head began to nod he was rudely startled out of sleep by a different kind of jerk. He had tied Zutu's halter around his wrist and suddenly it was yanked so hard that Carl felt the blood throb in his hand as circulation was cut off. Slightly dazed, his whole body was pulled forward and up with the strain, then the halter slackened. The horse was close to him, shaking his mane and dancing sideways. The shaggy coat had a peculiar glittery look. The sun had disappeared. It was almost dark.

Carl felt a pang of guilt. He must have slept longer than he thought. He must leave at once. As he emerged from the crevasse a blinding light, followed by a rumbling explosion that echoed throughout the valley, made him throw his hands over his eyes in fear. But he was not able to be frightened for long because it took all his strength to hold on to the pony.

"Zutu, it's all right. Come here, come here," he cried to the lunging animal—and then he felt it. It was no longer sweat that made his clothes stick to him. It was rain. Zutu had caught the first drops out there in the open, while Carl dozed unaware in the shelter of the crevasse. In response to his voice, the pony had calmed down and now stood quietly, while torrents of rain washed over Carl as he tried to climb into the slippery saddle. When he finally managed to hang on, he said, "Home, Zutu, back to Ácoma." A second deafening clap of thunder set the pony atremble and Carl worked quickly, speaking words of reassurance while he stroked the tangled mane. In a few moments Zutu recovered his poise, and even a zigzag of lightning shattering against Katzimo failed to stampede him.

"Let's go, Zutu. Back home now."

By the time they reached the base of Ácoma the torrential downpour had slackened to the kind of steady rainfall that the pueblo had prayed for. Carl knew that the crops could be devastated by too severe a deluge as easily as by drought, so the *k'atsina* had achieved perfect success. He and Zutu ascended the great rock in total darkness. Carl felt the tired pony laboring against the sticky mud, so he dismounted halfway up. Steadying himself against Zutu's flank, he slipped and stumbled along in the dark. The two of them had just slogged their way within a few feet of the top when Carl heard Wilbert's voice calling his name.

"That you, Carl?"

"It's me and Zutu. We're all right."

The mud-splattered pair blinked in the light of a lantern held aloft. Carl heard a gasp, then Helen said, "Cousin-brother, you look terrible! You must come home with me at once so we can take care of you."

"For a minute," Wilbert joked, "I didn't know which one was Zutu. But Helen's right, you'd better get to Aunt Plácida's real fast. I'll give Zutu a rub-down so he won't take cold. How did he behave?"

"He's a champion," Carl said. "I never could have done it with any other horse."

Helen motioned to Carl to come along, and he followed obediently, too tired to protest. As they climbed the ladder to Aunt Plácida's house Carl said, "The rain came, after all."

"Of course it did."

"Where's Horace?"

"He's at the other trail watching for you. Wilbert will tell him you're home. Hurry up. My mother has a pot of herb tea and some rabbit stew for you. Then you must go to bed."

9

The Race that
Nobody Won

There was a rock in his throat that he couldn't swallow and somebody kept putting cold knives against his back and legs. That went on for a long time. Then heat shot through him like a branding iron and an earthquake made him shake, shake, shake. Voices faded in and out but light hurt his eyes so that he couldn't keep them open long enough to see who the voices belonged to. He did hear a woman saying, "Ride over to San Rafael as fast as you can and tell them to bring the truck and take him over there. They have their own doctors and their own kind of medicine. They might not like it if we used ours."

After a while somebody helped him to his feet and people wafted him through the air and down a ladder. Then he was in some kind of vehicle and his mother was there. His mother was always there but his father only now and then and Leo too. After a while he began to ask what time it was and if it had stopped raining yet, but nobody would tell him and that made him mad. They were always saying "shh" and "go to sleep" and "take your medicine."

The first thing Carl asked when he opened his eyes and looked at the solemn faces around his bed was, "Did I nearly die?"

"As a matter of fact, kiddo, you didn't," Leo said. "You were plenty sick and for a while the doctor thought we might have to take you to the hospital in Albuquerque but your fever broke a lot sooner than it does with most people."

"What was the matter with me?"

It was Juana who answered this time. "Almost pneumonia but you're a strong and healthy boy and you managed to throw it off."

Carl tested his arms and legs, then sat up and reached for a glass of water. The room and the people in it slid to one side and his head wobbled to the other. "I still don't feel so good," he said.

"Nobody feels good after spending a week in bed except lazy good-for-nothings," Solomon said pompously, "and you're not one of them."

Suddenly Carl paused in the midst of a gulp of water. "Zutu! What happened to him? Did he get sick too?"

"He's healthy as a horse," Solomon assured him. "He and Wilbert brought the message to us that you were sick the morning after the rain dance. Now lie down again and your mother will get you something to eat. She made the best medicine in the world—

homemade chicken soup with noodles."

The room cleared of people and Carl lay there with that light, bodiless feeling of the convalescent. Scenes walked in and out of his mind—the ride on the plains when he and Zutu were one, the big black rattlesnake in the lava beds, the prayer stick he threw onto the ledge, Katzimo, tolerant but not welcoming. Then the door opened and his mother came in carrying a steaming bowl of soup.

"I'm hungry," Carl said. "Is that all I get? How about some tortillas or bread?"

"Tomorrow. The doctor said that today you can only have soup, milk, or fruit juice." Juana stayed with him while he ate. She sat quietly, then smiled at him when he got to the bottom of the bowl and said, "Gee, mom, that was good."

As she picked up the tray, she said, "Well, Carlitos, what happened?"

Carl was immediately on guard. "What happened? You know all about it. There wasn't much for me to do after the first few days of the Natyati so I asked Wilbert if I could go out camping with Zutu. I mean, Wilbert offered me—I mean Zutu and I, well, you know—" Carl began to run down because his mother was watching him with that calm penetrating look that saw right through everything to the heart of the matter.

"Was it Horace again?"

"Yes," Carl said reluctantly, afraid his mother would get it all out of him.

182

"I won't ask any more questions, don't worry. Lie down and go to sleep now."

"Wait a minute, mom. When can I go back to Ácoma?"

"Do you still want to?"

"It'll be my last chance before we leave for San Francisco."

"The doctor says you can get up tomorrow. You had a high fever but no complications. If you're all right in a week or so, you can return."

After his mother shut the door, Carl closed his eyes but it was a long time before he went to sleep. Katzimo and Horace kept running through his mind. Somehow, his cousin and the mesa had blended into a single formidable opponent. It was all a jumble in his head as he started to doze off, but he knew he had to go back once more because the pueblo was a part of him now. If he could understand Horace's rejection of him, would he understand Katzimo too?

In a few days Carl was able to help Solomon and Leo in the store. There was plenty to do because July and August were the busiest months at the trading post and many tourists drove through San Rafael, eager to see the Wild West, some of them still believing, in 1925, that buffalo roamed the plains and that they might glimpse a herd over the crest of the next hill.

One of the happiest events of that week was the return visit of Harold, Paolo, and Quate on their way to Mogollon. As soon as Carl saw the short squat figure climbing out of the back of the truck he began to grin. Racing out of the store past the astonished customers, he pumped Quate's arm up and down until the little man said, "Whoa, *chico*, you musta been lifting five hundred pound sacks of flour. Let go my hand before you crush it up like peanut brittle."

Since Harold was not in training for a fight, there was more opportunity to relax and have a real visit for a few days than there had been before. During the time the trio stayed at San Rafael, Carl drew out of Quate every tale he had ever known about lost gold mines, boxers ancient and modern, and ghost towns of the Old West. Solomon and Paolo, who both liked to spin a yarn themselves, yielded gracefully to the colorful storyteller. Leo cancelled several dates in Albuquerque so he wouldn't miss out on the entertainment at home, and even Juana asked Quate to delay his stories until supper was over, when she could be free to sit down and listen from beginning to end. Quate thrived in the spotlight. He acted out different roles in the stories he told and had them roaring at his imitation, falsetto voice and all, of the fat female owner of the biggest saloon in Mogollon.

Carl discovered that Harold had enjoyed another victorious fight since the one at San Rafael. During the visit he and Harold worked out a few times.

"You're doing better than you were a few weeks ago," Harold commented, "but maybe not as fast."

"I'll be in shape soon. Being sick set me back a little."

When it was time to leave, Quate delved into the back of the truck and came out with a parcel wadded up in brown paper. "It's for you, Carl," he said solemnly. "Something special, but don't drop it."

As Harold climbed into the front seat of the truck he called back, "For sure, don't drop it on Aunt Juana's clean kitchen floor."

Carl was standing beside the truck when it began to roll. Suddenly Quate leaned out and said in a low voice, "That other one, that *chico* Horace that ran back to Ácoma. Quate saw the way it was between you two. Instead of fighting him, Carl, why don't you give him boxing lessons? It's more better that way."

When Carl entered the kitchen he was carrying the package that Quate had given him.

"What's that?" his mother asked.

"It's a present from Quate."

Juana shooed him away with her apron. "You'd better open it outside. Who knows what kind of jokes Quate plays."

When Carl tore off the wrapping and held up the quart bottle he began to laugh.

"What's the matter? You off your rocker or something?" Leo shouted as he hurried by with an armload of fur pelts. "Come on. Some Navaho families are here and I need help." Then Leo paused, did a double-take, and called out, "Say, what is that stuff in that bottle anyway?"

"It's Quate's secret formula."

"What do you do with it?"

"You rub it on your hands."

"Do anything you want but don't drink it."

During the week Wilbert rode over from Ácoma on Zutu to see how Carl was but he couldn't stop for long. The harvest was beginning at the pueblo and all hands were needed in the fields. Horace didn't come and Carl didn't ask for him nor was any information volunteered. But before Wilbert left he asked Carl, "Will you come back to Ácoma and stay with us once more before you go home, cousin-brother?"

"I want to very much."

"Any time you are ready, we are waiting for you."

Shortly after this Carl was alone with his father on Saturday evening. Leo had driven off in his Ford to a dance and Juana was visiting across the street with the wife of Antonio Lavo, the blacksmith. The jangle of the old cash register had just died down and Solomon was clanking silver dollars into piles before sweeping them into felt bags when Carl said, "Papa, can I go back to Ácoma soon?"

"We have to go home in a few weeks. We'll all be going over there to say good-bye."

"I want to go and stay for a while, not just to say good-bye."

"Help me carry these bags to the safe in the back room, Carl."

Carl stood by while his father squatted down and twirled the dials on the safe. When the door was open he asked again, "Well, dad, can I go?"

With his head still inside the safe, Solomon's voice was muffled. "Are you sure you want to?"

"Why do you ask that? Because I got sick? I feel

great now."

"No, no, no, no." The last no was louder than the rest as Solomon sat back on his heels once more and shut the door. "I say it because—" Solomon shrugged his shoulders, "—because I say it. Are you sure you want to grow up some more or have you done enough growing up for one summer?"

"That sounds silly. I don't understand it."

"And I can't explain it. If you want to go back, yes, yes, you can go."

Monday afternoon Leo told Carl that he'd drive him to Ácoma in the pickup truck. They had a hard time getting under way because Juana kept thinking of something else she wanted to send Plácida and María. She had already told Carl to put a case of peaches and pears in the truck, knowing that canned fruit was a favorite at the pueblo, to be used on special occasions during the winter months.

"Do you want to take candy for Helen and the boys?" she called to Carl as he came inside.

"No, not this time."

"What about some of those licorice whips that you took for Horace?"

"I don't think so, mom. It's better to take something that everyone likes."

"Did you ever give them to him?"

"I gave them away to the pueblo children at the rainmakers' dance when everybody else was giving presents."

"Oh."

Carl was glad she didn't ask why. He scarcely knew

the answer himself, except that when he was actually with Horace it always seemed that a gift might be misunderstood as a bribe. If Horace wouldn't accept him for himself, he certainly wouldn't be impressed by a bag of candy. Quite the other way—he might even refuse it.

Juana put both hands on his shoulders and turned him around to face her. "*Hijo mio*, what you are thinking shows in your face. We cannot like everyone but we can try to understand them. I can see that you still haven't asked Horace why he acts the way he does. I won't mention it again but it would be good to know, wouldn't it?"

"Even Wilbert doesn't know, so why should Horace tell me?"

"Sometimes it's easier to tell a stranger than to speak to one close who sees you all the time."

Carl was saved from making any promises because Leo, passing by at that moment, called out, "Get on the other end of this box, Carl. Papa says the family should have a case of green peas too."

Right after lunch Leo drove Carl to Ácoma but the "city in the sky" was deserted, except for a few old people and babies. Everybody was out working on the plains, harvesting the corn crop.

"Let's put these things in the storeroom at Aunt Plácida's house," Carl said. "Then you can give me a lift to the fields and I can help with the work."

When Leo dropped him off, Carl didn't try to locate his relatives in the crowd of people spread out over many acres of land. He simply fell in beside the workers and assisted as best he knew how with the hot and tedious job. After he had worked for a while the boy in the row ahead looked back and said,

"Hello, *mutietsa*, boy, you've been away."

It was the big good-natured fellow who had wrestled the rooster away from him in the *gallo* race.

"Here, take this," the boy said. "You'll need it." Reaching into his overall pocket, he fished out a red *banda* like the one tied around his forehead. Carl accepted it gratefully. Drops of perspiration were already running down his face.

The boy was gathering corn with his bare hands. Neither knife nor reaping hook was in evidence with any of the workers. Within the hour Carl's hands were getting sore and he was afraid he would have to give up, but at this point his friend glanced back and said,

"Hey, *mutietsa*, Carl. That's your name, isn't it, cousin to Wilbert and Horace?"

"That's me."

"Your people are over there." The boy pointed across the field. "Better find them now so they can give you a ride back home. It's almost quitting time."

"Okay."

The boy immediately bent to his work but he called back over his shoulder, "Tomorrow we get a rest. We're going to have a whib race. You come too. Maybe you'll run with us."

"Thanks. I'll be there."

As Carl reached the far side of the field and spotted

Wilbert among the rows of workers, the sun dropped and, as though a buzzer had sounded, the people straightened up and the day's work was done.

"Hi, Wilbert," Carl called out. "I'm back again to stay for a while."

Wilbert waved and began to run toward him. In a moment he was joined by Helen, then Aunt María and Plácida. There was a great deal of jabbering and joking as they walked off the field together and Carl realized that it was all very similar to the way his mother and father had been greeted at the start of the summer. Now he was part of the family too.

On the ride back to Ácoma in the wagon, Carl sat next to Wilbert who was driving the horses. Suddenly a familiar figure galloped by. It was Horace riding Zutu. Carl called out to him but there was no reply.

"He didn't hear you," Wilbert said. "He was too far away."

"Even if he had, he probably wouldn't answer."

"Don't be hard on him, Carl," Wilbert said quickly. "He's been having a rough time."

"What do you mean?"

Wilbert shook his head. "I can't tell you but maybe he will."

"Fat chance."

"How long can you stay?"

"About a week. We have to get back to California for the start of school."

After Wilbert's plea for tolerance toward Horace, Carl made a silent vow to try once more to talk to his cousin that evening. Throughout supper Horace seemed more on edge than ever before and as soon as the meal was over he jumped up, mumbling his usual excuses about having work to do. Unlike the usual routine, Carl got up too, saying, "Wait. I'll give you a hand," and followed Horace out the door. But by the time Carl reached the porch his cousin had disappeared into the dusk. Carl began to walk the streets in search of him, but the only activity he encountered was a group of children playing a game of hidden ball, the pueblo equivalent of marbles.

He decided to carry his determination one step further by waiting on the roof of Aunt Plácida's house in hopes of intercepting Horace. He sat there until night shrouded the pueblo. With the dark came the knowledge that as long as he remained there, Horace would stay away, and Carl decided that there was no use fighting anymore. All he wanted now was to spend his remaining days at the pueblo in peace and quiet, enjoying the rest of the people he knew and liked so well.

Early next morning before the family awakened, Carl eased himself out the door and down the ladder to the street. Time was growing short and he wanted a last opportunity to watch Katzimo emerge from dead of night into living daylight. He also wanted to concede defeat before the mighty rock. He had finally admitted to himself last night that the ascent of Katzimo, that he had been so sure of when he first

arrived, was an impossibility for now. Sometime later, when he returned to Ácoma in years to come, he would accomplish his purpose.

He posted himself at the far end of the graveyard overlooking the valley. The darkness prickled with little shafts of gray. Then the night mists of Katzimo, caught in crevasses and impaled on crags, were slowly pulled away, as though some primordial treasure were being carefully divested of its protective covering. When the last tufts of mist streamed off and dissolved into light and air the citadel, bathed in rose-color, gave out thousands of tiny sparkles. It was like gazing into the heart of an enormous diamond. For the brief time it lasted, Carl was hypnotized.

"You are well now, my son. We are glad to see you back."

Carl was not startled. He knew at once who it was, and it seemed appropriate that his trance be broken by the voice of Lorenao Watshm Pino.

"Yes, sir, I am well." He turned and looked into the face of the cacique.

"And you are healed?"

It was an odd question and Carl didn't know quite how to answer. He was saved the necessity, though, because the cacique opened a small buckskin bag, took out a pinch of cornmeal, and scattered it on the earth before him.

"I have come to give thanks to *naiya h'ats*, mother earth, for the richness of the harvest." The cacique spoke a few words in the Ácoma tongue, then, putting the bag away in his pocket, he said to Carl, "You have only a few more days to stay with us. I may not see you again and so I want to tell you that we are sorry that you became ill, and we are sorry that you were driven from the Natyati by the hasty words of one of our young men."

"I—well—I guess it was as much my fault as his," Carl said lamely.

"Always remember that you are an honored guest who has also a right by birth to call Ácoma home at any time you want. Come back to us again soon." The cacique bowed his head and raised his hand in farewell.

Carl returned the salute and watched the straight unhurried figure make its way back to Mauharots, the head *estufa*.

Somehow Lorenao Watshm Pino was aware of the harsh words that had been spoken between himself and Horace. Perhaps this was what Wilbert meant when he said, "Don't be hard on him, Carl. He's been having a rough time." There was only one thing to do during these last days and that was to avoid Horace as much as possible. In this he knew he would have full cooperation from his cousin. When he couldn't avoid Horace, he must keep his mouth shut. Carl realized that he no longer wanted to fight Horace. The meeting with the cacique, his concern and his courtesy, had taken that desire away completely.

After breakfast Wilbert dropped by to pick up Carl and Horace for the whib race. As they walked

194

down the footpath Wilbert explained that this was an ancient contest between two teams of runners circling the base of the great rock of Ácoma and that he and Horace would be on one of the teams. Carl was invited to join in, too, but he had made up his mind that he would not participate as soon as he heard that Horace would be in the event. Any competition with his cousin could set up a situation where tempers might flare. As the three of them walked down the trail Carl said, "You'd better count me out. I'm not that good a runner. I wouldn't be much help to the side I was on."

Each team was composed of six members. The participants wore only a loin cloth and a *banda* around their foreheads, and all of them had painted their legs, arms, and torsos in the same designs and colors. The whib itself was shaped like a flattened banana and each group of barefoot runners had to keep this stick ahead of them with their toes as they ran a distance of some fifteen miles. In this, as in any other sport where speed and dexterity were essential, Horace could not be outdone by boys and men bigger and stronger than he, but Carl wondered if he had the endurance for such a lengthy race.

Just before the start, Wilbert offered Zutu as a moving chair from which Carl could follow the racers. Carl accepted eagerly because it gave him a vantage point over the heads of other spectators on foot who were strung along the route. During the first few miles the two teams shouted back and forth, joking and making comparisons about the prowess of themselves and the others. But as the contest went on and the contestants began to tire, their comments dwindled until the silence was broken only by grunts of exertion. The runners were a little more than half-way around the base of the big mesa when there came a sudden speeding up of action. As the pace increased, Zutu began to respond as he always did to competition, whether he was involved in it or not. He so obviously wanted to outrun the runners that Carl was forced to keep a tight rein, whisper soothing words in his ear, and use every bit of his newly acquired horsemanship in an effort to control the eager animal. By the time Zutu had calmed down and Carl was able to turn his attention back to the race there were only a few miles left before the finish.

As Carl scanned the team that his cousins were on he became alarmed at the change in Horace. Every rib on his thin chest stood out from exertion as he struggled for breath, and his eyes were blank with fatigue. All the runners showed strain, even older men long conditioned to contests that demanded superhuman effort from merely human bodies. But, although there were several boys no sturdier than Horace, his expression alone was one of true agony. It's a team sport but he thinks he's the only player on it, Carl thought. For him there's no pleasure in the game unless he wins. If his side loses he'll blame himself. Wilbert and the rest of them aren't like that. Horace is more Anglo in his thinking than he is Indian.

As the contestants approached the finishing line, Carl and Zutu skirted the crowd that was shouting the runners on as excitement mounted. Bets were being exchanged on all sides, and many a cherished necklace, horse, or saddle would be lost or won before the day was over. Carl, unable to take his eyes off Horace's face, became more frightened with each passing moment. The flesh was gray, the cheeks sunken like those of an old, old man. Horace stumbled so often that Carl knew he must collapse, and still he went on. His team was behind now. Several of the other runners on it were alternating in pushing the whib, but they were losing ground rapidly to the competition.

So certain was Carl that Horace would be flat on the ground in a matter of moments that his hand went automatically to his water bottle in readiness to give aid. But when he looked back he couldn't believe his eyes. Horace's whole body had straightened, he had regained his composure, and now he was regaining his speed. The gray look was gone, the eyes were bright and keen as they had been at the start. Now he looked fresher than anyone else in the whole contest and he forged ahead of his teammates, taking over the whib, his bare feet working so fast that his side was soon in a position to pass the other.

As the change became apparent to the people scattered along the last hundred yards, the crowd went wild. The other team began to pull up again and every runner in the race, on both sides, put forth his last ounce of reserve strength. It was neck and neck. Carl, guiding Zutu through the shouting spectators, kept glancing at Horace in disbelief. He was the lead runner. Lean and lithe, his movements were so rapid and smooth that he made the man he was opposing on the other team look clumsy as a mule. The crowd pressed closer. Carl was forced to maneuver Zutu out of the way to avoid trampling someone, so he missed the actual finish but he knew the grueling marathon was over because a gleeful shout of *"Ah-a-a-a Ai"* rent the air and pandemonium broke loose. The next moment there was a peculiar rumble of voices and Carl couldn't tell what emotion the sound expressed. Dismounting Zutu, he led him slowly through the press of people, trying to make his way toward the front. All at once he was wedged in and could go no further.

"What's happening," Carl asked the man nearest him. "Is something wrong?" But the man was too intent on peering over the shoulder of his neighbor, and the question went unanswered. Edging his way back out, Carl mounted the pony again and trotted around the outer fringes of the throng. Just as he reached a point where he could see the finish line, the heads of all the people turned to look upward. Following the gaze of the group, Carl saw three figures ascending the trail. Two men supported a third between them. The head of the center figure drooped forward, feet trailing in the dust. Someone was hurt. The crowd had begun to disperse, though little clusters of people still remained talking together, glancing at the three men who were almost at the top of the mesa now. As the group nearest Carl

198

broke up, he saw the big boy who had befriended him in the cornfield yesterday.

"Hey, there, what happened? It's me, Carl Bibo."

"Didn't you see the finish?" The boy's chest was still heaving. He had been one of the runners on the team opposing Horace's group.

"I was trapped in the crowd."

"Your cousin Horace was way out in front at the end. I've never seen anything like it, but just before he got to the finish line he collapsed on one knee." The boy spread out his hands in a gesture of finality. "Then he fell face down on the ground and didn't get up."

"Is that so unusual after a race like that?"

"No, it isn't, but he never did get up. They say that nobody could hear his heart beat."

Carl's heart began to pound at this ominous news. Digging his heels into the pony's sides, he headed for the top of the mesa. As he neared the end of the trail he could see Aunt Plácida's house in the distance. People were climbing up the ladder and there was a cluster of figures on the rooftop. The two figures, still carrying the third, detached themselves from the group and entered the door of the house, closing it behind them. Zutu picked his way slowly down the quiet street, seeming to sense that the noise of galloping hoofs would not be appropriate. Carl saw Wilbert descending the ladder. As he came to meet them, Wilbert said, "I'll take care of Zutu now."

"How is he?" Carl asked.

"We don't know yet. They've sent for the medicine men."

"He tried too hard," Carl blurted out. "You were one of the runners and probably didn't notice, but he looked awful, long before the race ended. Even the older men didn't push like that. Nobody should."

Wilbert shook his head. "It's not my way and it's not yours, but Horace is different. Something drives him, something we don't understand. You can stay at my house tonight, but you will be alone. It is the Ácoma custom for members of the family to stay with the sick one until he is cured. Horace's mother and father are not here this summer so Aunt Plácida, Aunt María, Helen, and I must be with him."

As Carl passed Aunt Plácida's house he saw a tribes-man climbing the ladder carrying a gourd rattle, an ear of corn, two eagle plumes, and some buckskin bags. Behind him were several elders bearing pottery bowls, a rock crystal, and small stone carvings of animals. Carl identified a mountain lion, badger, snake, and wolf. The men wore only breechcloths and they had painted a black band across their faces, covering the eyes like a mask. Their long hair was tied up in front with a strip of corn husk, and two short feathers were worn at each temple. Carl assumed that these were the medicine men, come to cure Horace. He hoped with all his heart that they would be successful.

There was no one at Aunt María's house. Some food had been laid out and Carl, not much interested in eating, helped himself to bread and fruit. At twilight he went out on the rooftop and sat down. The air was still, the sky clouded so that sunset was a slow, colorless procession of dreary grays that drifted into a charcoal night without stars. After several hours of the lonely vigil, his eyes closed and he drifted off into sleep. He was startled awake by a light touch on his shoulder and, looking up, he saw Helen standing there holding something in her hands.

"How's Horace?" he asked.

"He still doesn't talk or move."

"But he's alive?"

"Yes."

"What do the medicine men say?"

"They will work with him four days and four nights. If he is not better by that time then they will call in another curing society to give aid. There are four medicine societies and if a case is very difficult they help each other. They will do everything possible to drive out the disease. They will treat Horace with prayers and sacred herbs. Several times each year the medicine men walk all the way to a special place at the summit of Mount Taylor, twenty-five miles to the north of Ácoma, to gather herbs and roots. It is good medicine, cousin-brother."

Helen sat down beside Carl, then she said shyly, "I brought you a present that I made for you when you were sick."

Carl took the object that she handed him, then held it up so that he could see it better. "It's beautiful. I've never seen a bowl like it before."

"It's a *waititcani*, a medicine bowl," she explained. "Instead of being round it has four sides representing the cardinal points of north, south, east, and west. It is black and white because that is the tradition. Those are bear and cloud symbols that I painted on the sides. I must go back now, but I will be bringing, each day until Horace is well, some of the food we prepare at Aunt Plácida's house. Pray hard, cousin-brother. All prayers help."

After Helen left, Carl sat there for a long time holding the medicine bowl in his hands. Somehow the touch of it made him feel more hopeful that Horace would recover. When he went inside to sleep he put it down beside him on the floor. He slept restlessly, dreaming, at one point, that he and Mr. Lummis were climbing Katzimo. Mr. Lummis scampered up the formidable mesa with the agility of a monkey and stood on the summit shouting, "You can do it too, Carl, if you hurry up," but Carl could not even find a toehold to begin the ascent. Charles Lummis had been on his mind lately because he knew that he and his mother and father were going to stay at the Lummis home in Pasadena on the way back to San Francisco. Throughout the night Carl was aware of the muffled but persistent beat of the *tombé*. The constant rhythm had a soothing effect. Maybe it would also help to steady the heart and pulse of the sick boy. Maybe that was its purpose.

10

Saukin!

The day after the whib race there was still no change in Horace. When Carl saw Wilbert for a moment and asked about the sick boy, Wilbert said, "Horace hasn't moved or talked yet."

That evening, when Helen brought food to Aunt María's house, Carl blurted out, "How long can he go on this way?"

And Helen answered, "Until they cure him."

Carl was about to say, why don't you try a doctor in Albuquerque? But he realized it was none of his business. When he became sick the Ácoma relatives had taken him back to San Rafael to be treated with his own kind of medicine. Now that Horace was ill, they had a right to use theirs. But it was hard to wait for news, be so much alone and having nothing to do.

On the second day Carl began to wander, covering areas on the surface of Ácoma that he had never seen before. In a remote corner, far from the dwelling places of the town itself, he came upon a rock mound, built high with hundreds of tufted prayer sticks wedged in the cracks. He stood there looking at it a long time, then walked down the footpath to the base of Ácoma in search of scrub cedar. When he found some he broke off a branch and whittled a prayer stick. Returning to the place where he had found the rock mound, he carefully inserted the prayer stick into one of the cracks, saying silently to himself that it was for the recovery of Horace. Close by the rock shrine he found a cave with miniature bows and arrows and tiny parcels of sacred cornmeal tucked into its dusky interior. He disturbed nothing. With the exception of Horace's negative attitude, he had been treated with unfailing kindness in Ácoma and he felt that the least he could do was to show respect. He began to understand his mother's gentle ways and her tolerance of other customs and religions.

On the third day Carl spotted the ruins of a cliff house he had never noticed before, on a high rock above the southern portion of the mesa. The climb was such a rough one that it took him a long time to ascend, and when he reached the top it was close to sunset. He flopped down to rest on a ledge covered with ancient grit that was peppered with broken chunks of pottery, thorns, dried corn cobs, and nut shells. It was the most uncomfortable seat he'd ever felt, so he paused just long enough to catch his breath. When he stood up he saw Katzimo in the distance. It looked magic, like a solid mass of gold, the kind of treasure the Spanish conquistadors used to dream of finding. He knew it was only a trick of the sunset, but he stared at it, fascinated as ever. Then suddenly he felt his temper rise when he realized how many times, since coming to New Mexico, he had gazed in frustration upon this same glorious, unattainable sight.

Picking up fistfuls of dirt he flung them into the air while he shouted, "Katzimo, you're nothing but a bunch of dust and rock! What's so great about that?" Then he hurled a chunk of pottery in the direction of the mighty mesa and watched it shatter into fragments on the cliffs below him.

The only answer he received was that the sun disappeared and Katzimo turned a muddy brown with forbidding purple shadows at the base. He remembered Helen telling him that, for the Ácomas, these were the colors of death and witches. He began to scramble down from the cliff house. All the while he made his way back to Aunt María's, the thread of a plan kept running through his mind.

Early next morning he got up, stuck some bread and jerky in his pocket, and slung a water bottle and rope over his shoulder. Planning to be gone most of the day, he left a note so that if anyone came back to check they'd know he was all right. Counting back in his mind, he realized that this was the fourth day of Horace's treatment. Last night the usual food had been left for him when he returned to Aunt María's house. But since María and Wilbert were away again all night, he had to assume that Horace was still sick and that the family was continuing to maintain the customary vigil by his bedside.

The side of Katzimo that faced Ácoma was less than three miles away. Yesterday Carl realized that he had never really explored the base of the big rock and, although he knew it was impossible for him to walk all the way around in one day, he wanted to be able to say when he went home that he had scouted a portion of it. This was what he told himself anyway when he started out. He had just begun picking his way through the talus when it began to rain. It poured down in bucketsful, with brief intervals between as though water pails were moving from hand to hand, in an old-fashioned fire brigade, before the last man spilled the contents out. He had enough time between torrents to wipe the water out of his eyes, but not enough time to move to shelter before the next one flooded over him. The place he was in had no ledges to stand under, nothing to provide cover. Skidding and sliding through the mud, he tripped over pieces of rock as sharp as knives. He fell down twice, cutting his knee and tearing a hole in his pants. The minute he reached a spot where there was an opening that looked like a cave, the rain stopped.

Standing there, he got the feeling that it was all on purpose. It was another way for Katzimo to tell him to keep his distance. Soggy wet, with hair plastered down around his head, he knew that he looked like a crazy man when he turned and shook his fist at that solid mass of rock. He was glad nobody was there to see him. Seeking the shelter of the cave, he took off his clothes, wrung them out then wriggled back into them, figuring they'd dry faster on than off. He began to walk again, looking up and down the steep sides of the mesa, finally admitting to himself that he was looking for some place where he could make the beginning of a climb.

After a while he began to remind himself of a man he had seen once who trained dogs for the circus. The fellow kept holding up a hoop and, each time, the dog leaped into the air like he was going to sail right through it but he never did make it—at least not while Carl was watching him. Carl would keep seeing markings or ledges, and once a whole series of dark spots that went straight up the side of Katzimo to the top, but as soon as he came near they faded off into nothing or turned out to be shadows changing with the time of day.

It was late afternoon when he worked through to the southern end where he'd never been before. As he stumbled around a curve he suddenly came upon a big gorge or cove, cut like a V upside down into the body of Katzimo. A bell rang in his head and he remembered reading in *Mesa, Cañon and Pueblo* that it was a place like this where Charles Lummis had picked up the ancient trail that led almost to the top, and that it was the last thirty feet of sheer wall that made the climb so difficult. He also remembered that the problem had been solved by using an extension ladder, held by a man on either side and one behind for security, while Mr. Lummis climbed from rung to rung until he reached a point where he could be pushed over the top. But he knew that this knowledge wasn't going to do him any good because he was alone.

At this point Carl told himself that when he had started out in the morning he hadn't said anything like, I'm going to climb Katzimo. He was simply out for a hike because there was nothing else to do—so what? He turned his back on the big cold rock, took a swig out of his water bottle and tightened his belt, ready to go back to Ácoma. All of a sudden he turned right around, dropped the water bottle, and made straight for the gorge. He crawled about midway up the slope on hands and feet, then, as the going got tough and he looked up seeking a first handhold, he almost lost his balance and fell backward in surprise. There, plastered against the steep wall that led straight to the top of Katzimo, was a rope ladder, sand-colored against sand-colored stone, impossible to detect from the talus below because at a distance it blended into rough rock.

Carl must have stared at it for five minutes, trying to figure out who had put it there and if it had been there a long time. It was getting so dark that he couldn't see if it was fastened at the top or if it only went part way up. Was it rotted so that a person who tried it might drop down and smash into the jagged rubble? He knew there wasn't enough time left in the day for him to find out the answers. Even if he made it to the bottom of the ladder, he'd never get back to the sky city again by sunset and he was afraid somebody might report to the family that he hadn't come home for his supper. He didn't want his relatives to be worried about him with Horace sick, nor did he want anybody to know what he was trying to do. It was hard to leave but he knew he'd better come back at dawn the next morning, fresh after a night's sleep, ready to try again.

Ácoma was quiet as a grave when he got back at dusk. The few people he saw were disappearing into their houses for the evening meal. As he passed Aunt Plácida's house he could see no sign of activity, and when he climbed the ladder to Aunt María's it was the same as before. Nobody was there. Carl was so keyed up that he didn't feel tired, but he was hungry and it didn't take him long to see that food had been laid out and that there was a note placed beside the jug of goat's milk.

Picking it up, he read, "Dear Carl, Aunt Juana and Uncle Solomon sent a message that they have to leave sooner than expected because of business in San Francisco. They'll be coming to pick you up tomorrow at noon. You'd better gather your things together. I'll see you later. Cousin-sister Helen."

As Carl mopped up the gravy from his frijoles, he got the feeling again that every time he came close to doing what he had wanted to do all summer, Katzimo won and he lost out. No matter how early he got up in the morning, there wouldn't be time to make a try up that ancient trail to test the rope ladder, to see if it would hold and be back again ready to leave by noon.

During the course of the last few days either Wilbert or Helen had brought Carl's possessions from Aunt Plácida's to Aunt María's, so when he finished supper Carl began to stack his gear in a corner of the room. Picking up the medicine bowl Helen had made for him, he looked around for something to pad it with so it wouldn't break on the ride back to San Francisco. The minute he touched it his fingers began to tingle. It was the same sensation he had when his hand went to sleep and he felt prickles all over the skin. The bowl felt warm too, almost alive. It was as though it were sending a message to him. He put it down quickly on top of his clothes, afraid he might drop it. As soon as he let go, he knew what he was going to do. There was no other way and no other time. He had to do it now.

Once he made up his mind, he worked fast, not wanting any of the family to catch him before he left. He scrawled a note saying he was camping out and would see them in the morning, then he shot out of the house. There was a full moon coming up and he knew that would be a help. He took the long way round to get to the burro trail, not wanting to pass Aunt Plácida's house, in case any of the relatives might be coming out. When he neared the graveyard he saw people in the distance and heard voices, so he cut behind the church and through the corral where the horses were tethered. There was a high-pitched whinny that faded away as he ran down the trail. Carl knew it was Zutu because he had a funny way of putting a snort at the end of a whinny that was different from any other horse.

When he reached the base of Katzimo, he kept away from the talus and walked around on the plain until he came to the gorge where the trail was. The moon was ascending the sky now, bursting with white light. Even if I don't make the climb, Carl thought, it was worth coming just to see Katzimo. The gorge was bleached to the same silver as the moonlight, but on either side the big rock had turned to thick black velvet. It looked as though a spotlight had been deliberately focused on the ancient trail.

Carl paused, drinking in the sight, remembering the Ácoma legend of Kasewat, the great warrior and giant killer whose home was on the enchanted mesa. For a moment, the moonlight shivered into the shape of a man and he saw zigzags of silver and black war paint undulate along the powerful muscles of Kasewat as he climbed up and up, effortlessly, until he reached the top of Katzimo where Carl longed to be.

Carl shook his head to break the spell. Bending over, he started through the talus on all fours, feeling his way with his hands so he wouldn't fall or twist an ankle before he got where he wanted to be. When the rock smoothed out, and he was at the start of the climb where the slope was gradual, he stood up.

"Now," he said out loud. He didn't think of what a pygmy he was. He didn't feel scared because for the first time he thought maybe he could do it. Then it happened. The back of his neck prickled and a chill shot through his shoulders. Something or somebody was standing behind him. He didn't move and it didn't move, but he knew it was there all the same. He waited but there wasn't a sound. At last he whirled around and the two of them stood stock-still, staring at each other.

Carl spoke first. "Where did you come from?"

"From Ácoma, same as you."

"Did you follow me?"

"I was about to mount Zutu when you cut through the corral. Zutu whinnied and I was afraid you were going to see me, but I crouched down until you were gone. Zutu and I picked up your trail, but I stayed way behind so you wouldn't know we were there."

"I thought you were sick."

"I was, but when I woke up this morning I felt good as new and it was all over. The rest of the day we had ceremonies to give thanks because I was well. Nobody in the family leaves until they are over. Didn't you think our medicine men were as good as your doctors? Didn't you think they could cure me, or didn't you want them to?"

Horace hasn't changed a bit, Carl thought. He's as nasty as ever. "Why did you follow me?" he asked.

"I wouldn't follow you anywhere if I could help it. I had my own plans but it wasn't hard to figure out what you wanted to do."

"I don't get it," Carl said. "Listen, why don't you

run along back to Ácoma and leave me alone? Get a good night's sleep and maybe your disposition will be better in the morning."

"You've got it all wrong, the way you do with everything, cousin-brother." Horace stressed the last two words sarcastically. "You're the one who's going home. I'm the one who's going to climb Katzimo tonight. That's my rope ladder up there."

Carl took a deep breath, trying to hold his temper. "Why don't we both climb it?"

"No."

Carl tried another tack. "You were pretty smart to make that ladder." When he said these words he couldn't believe the change that came over Horace. He looked at Carl with such fury in his eyes that it was all Carl could do not to turn and run.

"Don't ever say that to me again!" Horace shouted. His thin face splintered and Carl was afraid he was going to cry. Then the whole thing backed up on Carl as he remembered the abuse he'd taken from Horace all summer long.

"Don't scream at me!" Carl screamed back. "It's always me who's trying to keep the peace. You can't even be decent the last night I'm here. Who do you think you are? I said you were smart to make that ladder. So you *weren't* smart. You were dumb, dumb, dumb—"

Suddenly Carl knew he'd better shut up fast because Horace started to cry. It wasn't like other people crying—it hurt to watch him because he was so ashamed of it. He half-twisted his body, turning his face away, putting his hands over his eyes. There wasn't any sound. That was the worst part.

Reaching down, Carl picked up his water bottle. "Okay, you win," he said. "After all, you've been pretty fair at that. You've let me know where I stand ever since I came to Ácoma. Sometimes I used to think you liked me, but then you'd change right back to hating." As Carl buckled the water bottle over his shoulder he realized that even if he had fought Horace and had beaten him so thoroughly that there was no question as to who was the superior boxer, it would have done nothing to fill the empty space inside him that Horace had created. Carl didn't even turn around to take a last look at Katzimo. He never wanted to see it again. He began to walk away, then paused and called back over his shoulder, "There's only one thing I want to know. Why was it such an insult to say that you were pretty smart to make that ladder?"

This time Horace didn't shout. Carl could barely hear him. "Because that's what *he* said."

"That's what who said?" Carl turned around and took a few steps back so he could hear the answer.

"It's not exactly what he said."

Carl walked up close to Horace. "You don't like me and that's okay, but there's got to be a reason."

"It's not you."

"All right. You don't like Anglos or even half-Anglos."

Then Horace began to talk. "When I was in school in Santa Fe I had a friend in town, an Anglo. We did everything together. We went fishing up the Pecos River, we hunted rabbits. Once in a while another boy would come along, a friend of his, an Anglo too. One day they were waiting for me on the street corner after school. They were talking and didn't see me when I came up behind them. I heard the other boy say, 'If you can't work that problem in your arithmetic book why don't you ask Horace?' and my friend said, 'Well, maybe I will. He's pretty smart—for an Indian.'"

They were both quiet for a while after Horace stopped talking. Finally, Horace said slowly, "I suppose you think that was a stupid thing to get mad at?"

"No, I don't. The half of me that's Anglo is Jewish. The other half's Indian. I've heard remarks like that on both sides. It hurts."

For a long time they didn't say anything more. Then Horace walked a few steps toward the gorge, put his hands on his hips, and stood looking up at the ancient trail.

"I was lying before when I said I was going to climb Katzimo tonight. The ladder isn't fastened. It's just hanging there. I borrowed Zutu because I wanted to ride over to see if it was still here. Before I got sick, I managed to toss it up a ways and it caught on a rough knob of rock. It would take two people to peg it in place. One would have to help the other from below." Horace looked back. His eyes met Carl's and, for the first time, each of the boys knew what the other was thinking.

"Let's go," Carl said. "It's my last chance this summer."

"You first. I'll back you up, tell you what to do, where to put your hands, how to fasten the ladder. You'll have to work holes in the rock before you can push the wooden pegs in. I carved some before the whib race. I've got them in my pocket. I brought a hammer too."

"How come, if you didn't plan to climb Katzimo tonight?" Carl asked.

Horace shrugged his shoulders. "It's hard to explain. There was this feeling—"

"I know, I had it too."

As they clambered up the incline Carl wanted to suggest that he be the one to back Horace up. Horace had been sick and he was so much shorter and lighter that Carl knew that if he slipped back on him, Horace would surely roll over and over down the slope and onto the sharp talus below. But he felt that this was no time to even hint that he, Carl, might be stronger, so he kept quiet. Suddenly a cloud slid across the moon, turning the night so black that for a minute Carl couldn't see a thing until his eyes adjusted. Good old Katzimo doesn't play favorites, he thought. He doesn't want me to climb him, but he doesn't want Horace either.

It seemed to take forever but at last they reached the ladder. Things went along slowly and smoothly at the start. With Horace handing him pegs and hammer in the dark, Carl was tall enough to be able to stand on the slope of the gorge, in relative safety, while he fastened the first few rungs into place. But soon he could reach no higher.

"Now comes the first hurdle," he said to Horace. "Let's see if it'll hold me."

"I'm right behind, backing you up."

Carl tried the first rung gingerly, with one foot, stepped on it, and climbed up to the second. The rungs held. "Now comes the next big test," Carl called back. "You'll have to move onto the first rung or you won't be able to hand me the pegs and hammer. Let's hope the ladder's strong enough for both of us."

Though Horace was light, Carl could feel the additional strain as Horace stepped on. There was the scrunch of wood moving against stone and the rung Carl was on quivered, then sagged, as a peg settled into place. But it stayed firm. Carl didn't realize he'd been holding his breath until he let it out with a whoosh and gulped another. "So far, so good," he murmured to himself.

In this torturous fashion—step by step, rung by rung—they climbed higher. Carl began to breathe a little easier. But when they got within a few feet of the top the thing happened. Suddenly Carl's hands seemed to swell into two big hams without fingers. He felt so clumsy that he was scared he'd drop the pegs down on the rocks below.

"Listen, Horace," he whispered, although there

was nobody to hear them, "do you have any extra pegs with you?"

"No, just the one you're holding now and the last one to go on the other side. Why? What's the matter?"

"I don't know for sure. I'm afraid I might drop one of the pegs. If I did, we'd be only a couple of feet short of reaching the top."

"Go ahead," Horace said. "It's got to be all right."

Carl fumbled the peg into the hole, hammered it in, and managed to slip the loop on the side of the rope ladder over it. One more to go. Reaching back, Carl felt Horace put the last peg into his hand.

"Here goes," Carl said. This peg didn't fit in easily. It jutted out at an angle. Carl had to hold it in place with his left hand so he could rap it with the hammer he held in his right. There wasn't much elbow room in the narrow crevice and it was almost impossible to swing with enough strength to drive the peg home. This time Carl wasn't afraid he'd drop the peg but that it might break in two because he couldn't hit it straight on.

It was getting colder. An icy wind slashed along the top of Katzimo and flung dust in his eyes. His hands were slimy with sweat, but he didn't dare wipe them off for fear he might lose his balance. Horace, on the rung below him, was absolutely motionless. Taking a firm grip on the hammer Carl whacked the peg as best he could, then tried it gingerly with one finger. It wobbled in the socket.

"I'm going to have to do it again," he warned

Horace, trying to keep a quiver out of his voice. "Hold tight."

The crevice was as dark as a cave. He couldn't really see what he was doing, he could only sense it. This time he was going to have to let fly harder and, to complicate things, he had begun to tremble. Maybe it's the cold, he thought, or maybe it's knowing that this is our last chance. He pushed away the sudden vision he had of the long drop down to the base of Katzimo. During his walk yesterday he had seen the bleached and broken bones of animals wedged between talus as sharp as dragon's teeth. Lifting the hammer, he drove down hard, then, carefully, with thumb and forefinger he tested the peg once more. It didn't turn in the socket. It was firm. He slipped the loop over it and said to Horace, "Let me climb this last rung, get on top. Then I can give you a hand up. I won't feel safe until we're both on solid ground."

In a minute he was sprawled out on the summit, hanging on to a boulder with one arm and reaching down with the other to Horace. They clasped hands, Carl pulled, and, thin as Horace was, he seemed to fly through the air.

They sat there side by side in the dark, breathing hard, waiting for their hearts to stop banging against their ribs.

"How do you feel?" Carl asked.

"Free," Horace said, then "light."

Carl knew what he meant.

"I had to do it," Horace said. "Not like you, just because you wanted to, but because every Ácoma boy must climb Katzimo."

"You mean it's part of a ritual?"

Horace nodded in the dark.

"I didn't know, or I wouldn't have gotten in your way."

"It's a good thing it happened." Horace didn't explain any further and Carl didn't ask him to.

Carl dozed for a while—he couldn't help it, he was so tired. At one point he woke up and Horace wasn't anywhere nearby. Carl figured that there must be certain ceremonies Horace had to go through—private things between himself, the spirits, and his ancestors. Hard though his bed was, Carl dozed off again and it seemed as though he had just closed his eyes when he felt a tap on the shoulder. Horace stood there in a world that glowed with rose-pink light.

Motioning to Carl, Horace walked to the edge of the mesa. Carl followed him and they stood together watching the day come alive. As the enormous valley yielded its wonders to the demanding light of day, it seemed to Carl that all the mysteries of creation lay revealed before him and that he and Horace were the first men ever to see them. I know there'll never be anything like this again, Carl thought. Even if I climbed Katzimo a dozen times, things like this only happen once. A tinge of sadness touched him and for the first time he knew the sense of loss that comes with the fulfillment of a cherished dream.

"Hold out your hand," Horace said abruptly.

Carl looked at him for a minute, then thrust out his hand.

Horace turned it over, palm up, fished in his pocket, then dropped two rough agate stones shaped like arrowheads in it. "I found them on the other side of Katzimo," he said.

Carl was about to say, I don't have anything for you, but he kept quiet. He could tell by Horace's face that he didn't want anything in return, that he only wanted to give something.

"Thanks a lot," Carl said.

At noon, when Carl's mother and father came to pick him up, the whole pueblo gathered at the base of Ácoma to see them off. As Carl walked down the trail carrying his suitcase, and saw the crowd congregated below, he had the awful feeling that he might bawl like a baby. It came upon him all at once and as soon as he had stowed his bag in the car he scurried around as fast as he could, shaking hands and mumbling good-bye without looking up.

It worked all right until he came to Wilbert and heard him say, "Too bad you can't stay until September second for the festival of San Estevan, the patron saint of Ácoma. But maybe, for this year, it's enough. Besides, it's always good to leave something special for next time. Then we'll be sure that you'll come back. We'll miss you but we'll be waiting for you."

Carl nodded his head, afraid to trust his voice. He

221

tried to put into his parting handshake the gratitude that he felt for all that Wilbert had done for him.

Even his uncles, Edward and Cipriano, were there, overalls splattered with bits of straw and adobe. Carl knew that they had taken time off from house construction to bid him farewell and they urged him to come back next summer when they would have time to take him hunting and fishing in the far reaches of the Ácoma lands, to places he hadn't been before.

He heard Solomon calling, "Come along, Carl, we have to get going."

As Carl hopped into the car, he saw the family up front waving, Horace at one side on Zutu. As the car started to go Zutu snorted, reared up, and lunged forward in pursuit. In no time he was galloping along beside them and Carl heard Horace yell, "Good-bye, cousin-brother. Good-bye, *saukin!*"

Turning to his mother, Carl asked, "What does that word *saukin* mean?"

"It's a good word," Juana replied. "In Ácoma language it means friend."

THE AUTHOR

BOBETTE GUGLIOTTA is a member of the Bibo family whose lives became entwined with the Ácoma Indians. Her first trip to New Mexico was in 1970 and was a journey of discovery. Her meeting with new-found relatives, Arthur and Nell Bibo in Albuquerque, disclosed the unusual family history upon which *Katzimo, Mysterious Mesa* is based. Later visits led to tape recordings with Harold, Leo, and Carl Bibo, the hero of the story, and to an acquaintance with the unique pueblo of Ácoma itself.

Bobette Gugliotta lives in Los Altos Hills, California. Her first book, published in 1971, was *Nolle Smith: Cowboy, Engineer, Statesman.*

THE ILLUSTRATOR

LORENCE F. BJORKLUND has illustrated numerous books, both adult and juvenile titles, and many of them have had to do with American Indians and the West which he knows so well. He has written and illustrated his own book, *Faces of the Frontier*, and collaborated with his daughter in preparing *The Indians of Northeastern America*.

Born in Minnesota, Mr. Bjorklund grew up in St. Paul. A scholarship to Pratt Institute brought him to New York, where he earned a living drawing illustrations for the then popular Western magazines. Today, he and his wife live in Croton Falls, New York, with summers spent in South Thomaston, Maine.